THE PORTRAIT

by

B.D. Anderson

Copyright © 2020 B.D. Anderson.

All rights reserved. No part of this book may be reproduced, stored, or transmitted by any means—whether auditory, graphic, mechanical, or electronic—without written permission of both publisher and author, except in the case of brief excerpts used in critical articles and reviews. Unauthorized reproduction of any part of this work is illegal and is punishable by law.

ISBN: 978-1-7346178-3-2 (sc)
ISBN: 978-1-7346178-2-5 (e)

Library of Congress Control Number: 2020904721

Because of the dynamic nature of the Internet, any web addresses or links contained in
this book may have changed since publication and may no longer be valid. The views expressed in this work are solely those of the author and do not necessarily reflect the
views of the publisher, and the publisher hereby disclaims any responsibility for them.
Any people depicted in stock imagery are models,
and such images are being used for illustrative purposes only.

All rights reserved.

This fantasy is dedicated to all my fellow IRAE Authors and the many readers who enjoy our stories. If you've ever visited a museum and stared at a beautiful painting wishing it would come to life, this story is for you.

Chapter One

MARLEIGH WALKED AROUND the yard sale with her mother, trying not to be bored out of her mind. Leah Winters loved yard sales, estate sales and any kind of sale, where she thought she'd get a bargain.

Marleigh couldn't understand her mother's fascination. After all, everything was used, dusty and old. Still, she loved hanging out with her mother and seeing the expression of pure joy on her face when she found a 'prize.'

At the moment, her mother was looking at some old dishes, depression glass, her mother explained, and it was no secret that Leah Winters loved to collect it.

Marleigh merely smiled at her mother's enthusiasm as she filled her basket with items while walking around the sale to see if anything else might catch her interest, though she doubted it.

She noticed some old paintings, sitting in their dusty frames lined up along the side of the owner's home. Walking over to look at them, her eyes fell upon a large portrait which had to be 20 by 24 in size. The frame was what first drew her attention.

It looked like and ornate baroque Victorian frame like the ones she'd seen often in the museum. Her eyes traveled to the portrait itself, of a man dressed in uniform, but she wasn't sure what branch of the military service he represented. He wasn't overly handsome, but his hair was the color of a new copper penny, though not quite as bright. Tall and well-built, sitting in a chair holding a sword in one hand and a tall fur hat in the other, both obviously part of his uniform.

His eyes drooped a little at the corners, while his lips were pressed together seriously. She felt like this young man, whoever he'd been, did not suffer fools lightly and most likely had been a good soldier. What held her attention most of all were his eyes. They appeared to be a combination of both blue and green. She'd never seen eyes like these. She couldn't stop staring at it and felt drawn to the portrait.

Marleigh moved in for a closer look, her face mere inches from the painting. Yes, his eyes were blue, but green near the irises. She didn't think anyone actually had eyes like this. The young soldier appeared to be looking at her with an unusual gaze, staring even as if he were sizing her up as she took in his features.

"It's not polite to stare," she mumbled aloud, though she knew she was doing the exact same thing. Was he now smirking at her? Impossible! She reached out and touched the frame. She leaned in closer for another look and was shocked when she felt a slight breath on her cheek. Probably a breeze. A portrait didn't have life. She backed up a bit. "I bet you were a hunk back in your day. Those eyes of yours probably broke many a heart."

"Marleigh," her mother called, walking over to her. "Did you find something?"

Looking away from the portrait, she turned to her mother.

Leah Winters could be described as a short and stout woman, a little under five feet with a short bob cut and no gray hair, but she carried herself with a commanding presence Marleigh couldn't deny. Her mother held a large wicker basket, now full of Depression glass.

"I was just browsing," Marleigh admitted, turning back to the portrait.

Her mother's gaze followed her daughter's hand as Marleigh caressed the frame. She stared at Marleigh in disbelief. "What is this?"

Marleigh could feel her mother's disapproval and drew herself up. "It caught my eye. I was wondering who he could be."

"It's just a portrait of some long dead person," her mother replied. "What would you want with that, and where on earth would you hang it?"

Marleigh laughed as her mother stared disapprovingly at the portrait. "Well, if it's not depression glass, I guess you can't see its value," she countered. Turning her focus back to the portrait, it appeared that the soldier in the portrait now glared at her mother. She quickly looked away, giving her mother her full attention.

"Maybe so. But I found my depression glass." Her mother glanced down at the basket she had on her arm. "I'm going to pay for it. I'll meet you at the car."

Marleigh watched her mother happily walk off, and turned back to the painting. "Don't mind her," she said running her hand along the frame once again. "She's not into art...or White boys."

Did his expression soften a bit? Marleigh couldn't understand why she felt compelled to talk to this painting. What was wrong with her?

"Young lady, I see you've found something," a voice said from behind her.

Startled, she quickly turned to find an older woman watching her curiously.

With white hair cut close to her head, she gazed at Marleigh with large brown eyes. "My father bought that painting years ago, and he used to talk to it also. I never thought anyone else would like it, much less talk to it like he did."

"I like it," Marleigh admitted, embarrassed. "I was just admiring it. I tend to talk to myself sometimes."

"Good, I'm glad you like it," the woman nodded, extending her hand to Marleigh "I'm Gertrude Wright. I know my father would have wanted it to go to someone who would enjoy it."

"How much?" Marleigh heard herself asking. "The details are exquisite. I didn't see an artist's signature."

"One hundred dollars," the woman replied looking down at a note pad she held in her hand. She pushed her glasses back on her nose. "No, I don't know who painted it. However, it does look a bit eerie to me. I don't look at it myself."

Marleigh sighed and shook her head. One hundred dollars was more than she could afford, though she believed this portrait was worth that and much more. She didn't think it was eerie at all. She glanced back at the portrait, and the soldier's eyes seemed to be pleading for her to reconsider.

"I'm sorry I don't have that kind of money," she responded, not sure if she was speaking to the lady or to the portrait. "I have to get back to my mother anyway. She should have paid for all that depression glass by now."

The older woman looked surprised. "That was your mother? Well, she certainly did buy a lot of items from me. I tell you what, since I can see you like the old boy, I'll sell it to you for twenty-five. I know Poppa wanted him to go to someone who would appreciate him."

"Really?" Marleigh responded surprised, looking at the portrait which seemed to now be staring at her with hopeful eyes. "I'll take it."

She was surprised at just how heavy the painting was when she picked it up. The car was only about twenty feet away, but she felt out of breath by the time she lugged it to her destination.

"Marleigh!" her mother gasped, apparently watching her approach the car as she struggled with the painting. "What in the world are you going to do with that young lady?" She eyed the painting distastefully.

Marleigh sat it down by the car. "I like it," she announced defensively. "I'm going to hang it in my apartment when I move there next month."

Her mother rolled her eyes, wrinkling her nose at Marleigh's purchase as she unlocked the car. "Really Marleigh, I knew you were a bit eccentric, but this is ridiculous, even for you. That picture looks like it's from the last century. I don't see the appeal."

Opening the rear passenger door, Marleigh pushed the painting into the car, onto the back seat as she responded patiently, "I wanted it because I like it, Mom. I haven't said one thing about all that depression glass you bought."

"Alright, you like what you like, and I like what I like," her mother said laughing at her daughter's frowning face. She swiftly kissed her cheek.

"Exactly!" Marleigh agreed, laughing.

FOR OVER EIGHTY YEARS, he had been trapped inside the painting. Winston wondered what would become of him now, since he was in the hands of a new owner.

His former owner, Miles McGregor had won him in a game of whist. How humiliating was that? Still, Miles had taken him home and began conversing with him as if he were a real person and not just a painting. Winston then found out this was the key to temporarily escaping his permanent prison. If someone believed he was real, then he had a chance to escape, even if it was only for a short time.

He had not known how his spirit had ended up in a painting to begin with and it was Miles who had filled him in as best he could. Winston remembered all of his past up until he'd been commissioned into Her Majesty's service in 1895 at the age of twenty-one. Queen Victoria was the Sovereign at the time. His next memory was waking up from a dream and being in this portrait of himself.

A woman named Temperance identifying herself as a witch, talked to him and told him that she was responsible for his current predicament. At first, he thought she was daft; crazy as a loon, but then she had cried out, *"Winston come forth,"* and he found himself removed from the painting and standing right there in front of her.

He remembered her cackling with glee, proclaiming that her spell had worked. She then explained how the portrait had been purchased from his mother's estate shortly after her death in 1921 and he now, belonged to her.

Winston quickly learned that asking questions of Temperance only irritated her and that once she walked out of the room, he'd be back in the portrait once again. Therefore, he listened to her when she called him out and eventually, he learned some of the answers to his unasked questions.

Temperance explained the rules. He couldn't be more than six or eight yards from the portrait and he would be sucked back in. If she left the room, he indeed would be pulled back in. Truly, her prisoner. He realized Temperance was just a lonely old woman who wanted a young robust man to gaze upon.

When she became ill, her son had used him as collateral in a game of whist and lost him to Miles McGregor who was leaving for the states the following month. Miles had wrapped him in brown paper, essentially sentencing him to darkness until he hung him in his home in America.

Finally, when Miles began talking to him, his hope of escaping his prison even for a short time was renewed. He had felt astonished when Miles had called him forth just as Temperance did when she had first cast her spell.

A tall man with dark hair and a thick mustache, Miles' green eyes twinkled at Winston's shocked expression when he stood before him. "You didn't think I'd take that bet from that arse without me believing you were worth one hundred pounds of my good money, did you? I knew Temperance was a witch and I purchased her diaries from that son of hers for ten pounds a month before I bought you. He told me that his mum believed that she'd cast a spell on the portrait, and that you were a real person. That boy of hers never took her seriously, never believed she was a witch; but I knew better. I've seen some of her handiwork."

"Really," Winston asked intrigued. "Has she done this before?"

"I am not sure about that," Miles had admitted. "However, I did see her actually reverse a fire once. The building was burning and the next thing I knew, the fire started burning in reverse until the house was totally restored. I knew then that gossip about her being a witch was true. It took me a while to figure out how to call you out, but I did. I had to consult another witch and pay her twenty pounds for the information."

Winston's response was to bow. "I appreciate any time I can actually escape my prison and move around," he had said.

The years had flown by for Winston while in Miles' company. His owner had been a widow with a young daughter at the time, and Winston could tell she was not the slightest bit interested in her father's portrait. He had been glad when she got married and moved out, but worried what she would do with him once her father passed.

Now, this young Negro girl had purchased him, and he had felt surprised when she seemed to have no problem talking to him. He could immediately feel a connection between the two of them which seemed much stronger than the one he'd had with Miles. Maybe there was hope for him.

The girl's mother had eyed him with distain, and he knew he was just another old and useless portrait in the older woman's eyes. However, the young lady named Marleigh had come to his defense. She liked him and called him a heart breaker. He felt something stir inside of him when he saw her, something he hadn't felt in years. A comely specimen of womanhood with full lush breasts and an ample bum that he knew would overflow his large hands. Her brown skin glowed under the heat of the day as she had struggled to get him into the vehicle. Her hair, a brown mass of wiry ringlets, worn loosely about her shoulders nearly sparkled under the sunlight.

Yes, Winston felt as if this Marleigh could make his bleak future a little bit brighter. Maybe once she took him to her own residence... he could once again, escape his prison.

Chapter Two

MARLEIGH FELL ONTO the bed, exhausted. She told herself it would be years before she moved again, because moving was just too much work. She hadn't acquired that much stuff, since this was her first move. What would it be like when she moved again, with more furniture than she had now? She groaned at the thought.

Still, she felt happy to finally be out of her mother's house. At twenty-four, she had a steady job at the Children's Museum and now, her own place! She sat up on the bed. She still had a lot more work to do, unpacking especially. She only owned a bedroom suite that she'd purchased for herself last year. Lucky for her, she'd had help from her father and uncle with taking it down in her old room and reassembling it here in the apartment.

Her mother had purchased her a kitchen set, and she felt this was all she needed right now. The living room could wait. After all, she wasn't planning on having anyone over anytime soon. The place wasn't big enough anyway with only one bedroom, but it was just right for her.

She got up to open boxes, removing her clothes and placing them in the walk-in closet. She glanced down and saw her father had placed the portrait of the soldier in the closet.

Marleigh grabbed it by the frame and quickly pulled it out. Her father told her the same thing as her mother had... he couldn't understand why she'd bought it, and she'd just grinned at his puzzled expression. He then joked that if this would be the only man she would have in her apartment; he could live with that.

Marleigh now noticed something scribbled on the back of the portrait that she hadn't seen before. The writing looked small and written in pencil.

She turned on the light and moved it closer. The writing looked faded and hard to decipher, so she reached in the drawer of the nightstand and pulled out a magnifying glass. She held the glass close and then backed it up a little. 'Winston,' it read.

"Winston?" she questioned aloud. "Could that be your name?"

She immediately turned the portrait around. "So, I know your name now," she said triumphantly. "It's Winston. How do you do?"

Winston's droopy eyes seemed to light up and his lips appeared to have a slight grin.

"Ahh, so you are Winston," Marleigh said, satisfied. "If anyone else was in this room and heard me talking to a painting, you know I'd be shipped off to the crazy house, right?"

Winston stared back at her.

She sighed, glancing at her weary reflection in the mirror that hung on the back of the bedroom door. "I should get out more. I'm actually talking to a portrait." Setting Winston against the wall, she stood in front of the mirror and stretched, leaning from one side to the other with her arms above her head. She glanced over at the painting. "I'll hang you tomorrow, Winston." She yawned and stretched again, while touching her toes.

"For now though, I'm going to shower and go to bed. I have a full day's work tomorrow." She glanced at Winston's stoic features and shook her head. What was wrong with her? Why did she feel compelled to explain her actions to a painting? Heading into the bathroom, she turned on the shower. Her muscles ached from the move and a hot shower was just what she needed.

Afterward, she came out of the bathroom wrapped in a towel to rummage through the chest of drawers for a night gown and panties. She sat on the bed naked and began moisturizing her skin, humming as she completed the task. She then stood facing the mirror and slipped a nightgown over her head.

Sitting again, she pulled on the panties before glancing at the ever-staring Winston. "You weren't supposed to be looking," she scolded, wagging her finger at him. "I bet you never saw a full-figured black woman before, hmmm?" She winked at the portrait. "I hope you got your eye full." Getting under the covers, she snapped off the light. "Goodnight, Winston."

Sometime later, Marleigh knew she was dreaming because she found herself at the yard sale with her mom again. She was with the same little old lady who was telling her about her father, talking to the portrait. Looking around, she then found herself in her new apartment with her father and uncle, moving her things around. She watched as her father placed Winston in the closet and shut the door.

She then found herself in the bed in her darkened room. She also knew someone was in the room, but she wasn't afraid. She reached for the light and blinked when she turned it on.

Winston stood there in full regalia with his hand to his brow in a salute, by the portrait that was still on the floor where she'd left it. He then lowered his hand and removed the furry hat from his head.

It reminded her of the water buffalo hat worn by the Flintstones in the cartoon, but this was no cartoon standing before her. "Winston!" She gasped while bolting upright. "What are you doing here?"

He was smirking as he walked over to her. "You purchased me, re-member?" he replied, his accent unmistakable.

Marleigh stared at him in disbelief. "Are you British?"

"Of course, and you are a Yank no doubt," he replied as he squared his shoulders.

Marleigh felt his perceived superiority. "I'm an American if that's what you mean," she replied crisply.

"That is what I said, Yank," he responded.

"We're in America, so yes, I'm an American and I bought you from an American, so get off your high horse," Marleigh snapped defensively.

"My former owner was British," Winston pointed out. "He moved across the pond to seek his fortune here in the Colonies. Of course, I had no choice but to come along."

"And now you're mine," Marleigh smirked. "I guess that's what got you worked up, huh?"

"Possessive, I see," Winston responded dryly, looking down his nose at her. He gazed around at the room and then back at her. "Well, it seems that you are proud to have any man in this bedroom, other than your father."

"You're an ass!"

"Yes, so I have been told," Winston replied, taking her hand and kissing it. "Winston Spencer, at your service ma'am."

"My name is Marleigh Winters," she said, withdrawing her hand. His lips had been soft and warm against her skin. The warmth traveled up her arm and made her stomach jump.

He kept smiling at her.

She then realized he'd been teasing her before. "I know I'm dreaming," she heard herself say.

"Are you really?" Winston raised a brow. "Why did you buy me?"

Marleigh glanced over at the portrait which sat on the floor and then back at Winston who stood by her bed. "I liked what I saw," she quipped saucily, trying to hide her nervousness and confusion. The portrait looked the same, but this man from the portrait now stood next to her bed, conversing with her like it was the most natural thing in the world.

"I must say that I liked what I saw when you came out of the bathroom with your arse bare," Winston replied winking as he sat down on her bed.

Scooting back, she pulled the covers up to her neck. "Winston, are you planning to take advantage of me," she asked giving him the side eye. "Is that even possible?"

"I am a gentleman," Winston replied coolly. "I do not take advantage of unmarried virgins."

Marleigh sputtered and coughed. "Who says I'm a virgin?"

Winston grinned at her as if she were an idiot. "Am I wrong?"

"That's none of your business sir," she replied haughtily.

"Of course," Winston conceded, nodding at her, yet still grinning.

Marleigh reached out and touched his arm. "What type of uniform is this?"

"I was part of the Fourth Queen's Hussars at Aldershot," he replied.

"You're an Army man?" Marleigh asked surprised.

"Yes." Winston nodded.

"How old are you?" Glancing down at his hands which were folded, she noticed he wasn't wearing a ring.

"Twenty-one." He stood, straightening his clothes. "I have been trapped in that damn portrait for years! I would like to get out and see how the world has changed, but there is no possibility of that."

Marleigh felt surprised at his sudden anger. "Why not? Why can't you go and see the world?"

"Because." He turned to her while speaking in his clipped British accent, "I cannot leave the portrait. I cannot leave this room unless you place it in another. I must always be close to it. I suppose I ought to be glad that I am living. That is...if that's what you call this?"

"What year was the portrait painted?" Marleigh asked.

"In the year of our Lord, 1895," Winston replied, glancing at his image in the painting.

Marleigh sat back against the headboard, dumbfounded. "That was over one hundred years ago."

Winston raised a brow. "I believe I heard someone say at the auction that this is the year 2019. Is that correct?"

"Yes, yes... it is."

"Yes, well then that makes me one hundred and forty-five years old," Winston concluded. "I am sure the world has changed quite a bit since my time."

"Yes, it has," Marleigh admitted. "Do you know how you came to be in the portrait?"

"It seems, this daft woman who many in my hometown of Oxford-shire, South East England believed to be a witch of some sort, cast a spell on me. This witch purchased the painting from my mother's estate. Apparently, she was enamored with my image and conjured me back from the dead, and so here I am."

"Do you remember your life before you were in the painting?"

"My memory is limited up to the time of the painting. I know I had a life...a long life in fact, according to my previous owner before you, but I don't remember any of it. I remember looking from the portrait to the woman, Temperance who I discovered was the witch. I was trapped in there until she uttered, 'Winston *come forth,*' and I then materialized and found myself standing in the hall where I was hung. I could only remember my early life until I'd been commissioned into Her Majesty's Service. Temperance told me that the spell removed any memory after the portrait was painted. She thought it was best. Anyway, she died and I was sold again and brought across the pond."

"Weren't you angry?" Marleigh asked.

Winston gave Marleigh an intense stare. "I do not dwell on that. You are the first person who has talked to me in years. I thought I would never get a chance to leave that portrait again. I know you think that you are dreaming, but if you ever want to see me again, all you have to do is say, '*Winston, come forth*' and I will be here."

"Did you come forth for that woman's father?"

"Of course," Winston replied. "However, he believed, but his daughter did not. Therefore, I could not come out once he died. All she could see was an old painting." He sighed. "So here we are. I suppose you will wake up and think this was just a dream, and I'll just sit, stuck in the portrait until you place me on some bare wall or back in the closet."

Marleigh yawned and stretched. "Oh, ye of little faith," she murmured.

"Get some sleep," Winston said. "I will be here. All you have to do is call me."

Marleigh looked at him as he walked back over to the portrait, touched it, and then disappeared.

All of this was very strange... Marleigh contemplated all of what he'd said. Suddenly, she felt tired and pulled the covers up around her neck before drifting off to sleep.

WINSTON HAD BEEN EVER so glad when Marleigh had removed him from the closet her father had stuck him in.

He remembered how her father had glanced at him and shook his head. "That girl of mine, sometimes I don't understand her," he'd proclaimed to his brother.

Winston knew that they were brothers because their features were very similar.

"Harvey, leave the girl alone," his brother had grunted. "Be grateful that it's not a real white boy, she's bringing in here."

Winston wondered what they had against Whites, but then again, he remembered that Negroes had only been free thirty years when he had his portrait done. He doubted they had been treated fairly when they obtained their freedom. Still, she did not seem to hold his race against him. He felt relieved about this too. His father had taught him that English speaking Anglo Saxons were superior to other races. Nordicism as it was called, a belief by the majority of British people, proclaiming they were superior and all races should be separate. He had never given it much thought until he joined Her Majesty's Service and began to travel.

Shortly before his portrait was painted, he had gone to Cuba to observe its war of independence and he secretly questioned his father's belief of Anglo racial superiority. The people in Cuba were smart and resourceful. Winston had realized that they were just as good as anyone else. He had learned much during his stay in the Queen's service as a lieutenant, and now he wished he could remember more.

He returned his attention back to Marleigh and had to admit to his attraction for her. He wasn't sure what he could do about it. What would a woman want with a 145-year-old ghost?

He had listened as she talked, and admired her naked form when she'd finished her bath. All woman, this one was. Yes, she was a Negro girl which would not be acceptable in his day, but what the hell! His day was long gone now. He had watched the telly with Miles enough to know that times had changed somewhat. Now he needed for her to somehow, to call him forth.

He had learned from Temperance years ago that if his owner dreamed about him, he could invade those dreams. He realized it might be his one chance to be able to communicate with her. Neither Temperance nor Miles had ever dreamed about him, but he felt himself being drawn out of the portrait as she slept. So he knew she indeed, dreamt about him. Her energy drew him to the bed where she slept and she opened her eyes. He could tell she wasn't fully awake, and when she pulled the covers up to her neck and turned out the light, he found himself back in his portrait prison once again. He could only hope that once she was fully awake, she would remember their conversation and call him forth.

Chapter Three

A WEEK PASSED AND MARLEIGH couldn't bring herself to believe the dream she had was real. A part of her wanted to tell Winston to come forth, and a part of her was afraid.

Winston seemed to stare patiently at her from the portrait while she took it and hung it on the wall beside her bed. She thought about putting him in the living room and then changed her mind. No, she felt he belonged here and this was where he preferred to be.

Could he really come to life? She remembered their conversation and even as he stood there by her bed, the portrait hadn't looked any different. She half expected the frame to be empty when he came forth, but it looked exactly as it had when she'd bought it.

"It was all a dream," she heard herself saying out loud. She glanced over at Winston who seemed to be smirking at her.

Marleigh wondered what would happen if she did say aloud, *Winston, come forth?* Nothing would happen, of course. It had all been just a very vivid dream. Still, it had seemed real and she could still remember his voice and his sexy British accent.

"Winston, come forth," she said aloud while eying the portrait.

Nothing happened.

Rolling her eyes, she walked over to it. "I knew it was all a dream."

"You sound disappointed."

She quickly turned.

Winston stood there, leaning against the bedpost.

"How did you get here?" she asked, startled.

"You called me forth," Winston replied. "Or don't you remember? I was hoping you would. I was beginning to doubt. It has been a week, Marleigh."

Marleigh stared at him as if he were a ghost. The way he said her name, all soft and sexy made her stomach jump. "Am I dreaming now?" she asked. "Are you real?"

"Are you?" he countered. "Dreaming, that is. I know you are real."

"No, I'm not dreaming." She moved over closer to where he stood. "So, you are really here?"

"I am," Winston said grinning.

Marleigh backed up and sat on the bed. "This is all so strange." She couldn't believe he was actually a real man, but he looked real enough. She watched as he moved closer, their eyes locking. Those gorgeous blue green orbs softened and he gave her a slight smile.

She noticed Winston was watching her closely and she couldn't look away. She could smell him, not recognizing the scent, but liking it. She wanted to run her fingers through his copper colored hair, but resisted the temptation. "So...I'm sure you have questions."

"It seems to me that you are the one who should have the questions," Winston replied.

Pausing for a moment, she wondered what his impression of her might be. Being from another time, did he see her as a person or merely an animal, less than human? "Are you upset that you're owned by a black girl...a plus size black girl at that? Would you have liked someone like your previous owner?

Instantly, the smile left his face, replaced by a look of confusion. "Why does that matter?" His brows drew together in puzzlement. "I have waited years to make a connection with someone. I could care less about your race or sex."

"But you're from 1895, our people were slaves—"

"Yes, yes," Winston cut her off. "We Brits abolished slavery long before you Americans. Bloody fools in the colonies thought that they could have free labor forever. We Brits came to our senses a lot earlier."

"But you Brits are snobs," Marleigh countered. "You look down on people."

"Well, not because of their color." He shrugged. "It's class. Not color."

Marleigh shook her head. "Well, I do not have a title or anything like that, you know."

"Yes, well that does not matter," Winston replied patiently. "You're a bloody Yank after all. I do not have a title either. My father was a second son. So, I am the son of the spare. Also, my mother was an American. I'm as common as they come." He walked over to the window and looked out. "I would love to go outside. It looks like a nice day."

"It is," Marleigh agreed. "We can go out if you like?"

Winston shook his finger at her. "The rules, my girl. The rules."

Marleigh walked over to the wall, picked up the portrait and headed to the door.

"What are you doing?" Winston asked surprised, following her.

"Taking you outside," Marleigh replied grinning as she headed down the hall.

WINSTON HAD BEEN DISAPPOINTED the day after her dream when they had talked and she hadn't called him forth. Neither did she call him the day after that. Now a whole week had passed, and he had lost hope. Was she afraid? Was she in denial? He realized also, she had not dreamed about him anymore, since he wasn't able to leave his prison again. He knew he just had to be patient, but it was hard.

He had watched her for a week. Every night she'd come out from her bath and rubbed herself down. He had found himself hard and aching, yet he could not look away. He knew her ritual. She would start with her feet and work her way up. He watched as she caressed her bum, then her stomach. When she reached her breasts, he thought he would explode with need. It had been pure torture, but such sweet torture.

He then felt truly surprised when she finally walked up to him, examining the portrait and running her fingers along the edges of the frame like she always did, saying the magic words. He found himself standing behind her at the foot of her bed as she continued to gaze at the painting.

He had not meant to startle her, but she visibly jumped when he had spoken.

She stared at him with those large brown eyes. A gaze he knew he could drown in, but he could not look away. He had been amused when she'd asked him if he cared about her being a plus size Black girl. What did that mean anyway? And by plus size did she mean...larger than normal? In his day, women weren't thin. This woman however, with her hair in tight spirals and those full, kissable lips, she was irresistible to him. He'd been lusting after her for a week. He now felt a stirring in his loins and hoped his arousal wasn't visible with the tight uniform he wore. He needed to rein in his passions, because after all, he was a gentleman.

He responded to her queries, even though his mind kept wandering; her scent of the cocoa butter lotion he learned she used to massage her skin, completely distracting. She was now talking about slavery and was calling him a snob!

He grinned at her. She wore a pair of tight jeans and he realized the Germans had invented those, but now every person seemed to wear them. Women in his day hadn't worn jeans. Oh, what he had missed out on in his young life. He tried to distract himself from perusing her frame and walked over to the window.

What he viewed was a beautiful, sunny day and he'd yearned to go outside. He had never been outside since he had been spellbound. Sitting on the grass as a portrait did not count. He figured there was no use wishing for the impossible. But he did say it aloud, he would love to be out there in the sunshine.

Winston had been startled when she'd offered to take him out, then watched as she headed down the hall with his portrait in her hands. He had instantly followed her, but he had not been quick enough, as he found himself back in the portrait once again.

Yes, he knew one thing now. Miss Marleigh would surely make up for the last eighty years of boredom.

Chapter Four

MARLEIGH TOOK THE PORTRAIT outside and sat it under a tree on her apartment grounds. Then went inside and made some sandwiches placing them along with chips and water in an insulated lunch bag. The day seemed quiet. Being a weekday, most people were at work while the kids were in school. The apartment complex was situated back from the street, and her apartment faced the now empty parking lot. Yes, it looked like a perfectly beautiful day.

She turned to the painting as it sat under a nearby oak. "Winston, come forth."

"I say, it is nice out."

She jumped, turning around to stare at him.

Winston stood behind her while looking around, wearing his fur hat and carrying his sword. He appeared completely entranced by his surroundings.

"Stop sneaking up on me," she protested.

He grinned at her turning his face up to the sun.

Watching his every move, she noted how his copper hair seemed to shine. Her gaze moved down along his face and for the first time she noted how his plump bottom lip protruded a bit while his top lip formed a perfect bow.

"I have not been outside in.... well I do not know how long," he said sitting in the grass and leaning with his back against the tree. Carefully, he took off the hat and sword to place them in the grass.

"Can others see you?" she asked worried, glancing towards the parking lot. "I don't want someone to call the cops and have me put in the looney bin because they think I'm talking to the air."

"Oh, they can see me," Winston said grinning. "However, you will have to explain why a Brit is sitting on your grass, in a uniform from the 19th Century."

Marleigh sighed in relief. "I'm not worried about that. We're in Washington, DC. People will think that you're a part of a reenactment or something. There's even a movie being filmed, I think."

"Excellent!" Winston said clapping his hands. "So now, what are we going to do?"

Watching his excitement, she found herself smiling.

He pushed his hat and sword aside to lay back in the grass. "Miles' daughter never saw me outside of the portrait. I believe the old boy wanted to keep me totally to himself." His face grew sad for a moment as if he was thinking of something, but it passed swiftly. "I cannot thank you enough for this little outing." He sighed in obvious pleasure. "I have not felt or smelled grass in years."

Marleigh studied him as he ran his hand over the grass and stared up at the sky; things she took for granted. He picked a dandelion and quickly blew it, sending the white seeds through the air, and she couldn't help but to smile even wider. "I was thinking..." She moved closer to him. "Why don't we go for a ride in my car? I can show you the city. We can put the portrait in the backseat and you shouldn't be pulled back into it."

Winston stood up. "Splendid idea," he said sounding excited. "I have watched the telly while in the portrait in my previous owner's bedroom. After he died, old Gertrude put me in the attic and there has been nothing but darkness for me until that yard sale. I would love to see your nation's capital."

His words disturbed her. She didn't like the idea of him being in total darkness. "How long were you in the attic?"

"I have no idea. I lost track of time with nothing to measure it by. Every day was the same and there were no windows up there. I have a lot of catching up to do."

Marleigh lugged the painting to her 2018 Jeep Compass with no help from Winston.

"I cannot touch it," he insisted apologetically. "It will pull me back in." He climbed into the car.

She got in the driver's seat, and quickly adjusted the rear view mirror.

"I say," Winston exclaimed wiggling in his seat. "This is a rather small motor car." He placed his hat and sword in the backseat.

Marleigh reached over and secured his seat belt.

He pulled on it curiously, examining it.

"For safety," she explained. "It's the law."

"Well, we cannot knowingly break the law and have the Bobbies on us now, can we?" Winston chuckled. "I say, it is rather a tight fit here! My head is touching the ceiling, and my knees have no room."

"I can fix that," Marleigh said while starting the engine. She reached across him and pulled the lever, instructing him to push back for more leg room. She then showed him how to recline the seat to be more comfortable.

"Well, this is much better," Winston replied as he adjusted himself.

Marleigh pulled out of the parking space. "Have you ever driven?"

"Oh no...I would catch the tram from time to time, but mostly I rode my horse."

"Tram?"

"It is sort of like a train...but on rails going through the city," he explained. "Of course, I was partial to horses. I loved to ride."

Marleigh drove around Washington DC, pointing out the sights for Winston who had a lot of questions.

"I believe your President was Grover Cleveland when I entered Her Majesty's Service," Winston said pointing to the White House.

"Boy, you are old," Marleigh teased.

"I carry my age well," Winston countered, winking.

After sightseeing another hour, Marleigh parked and reached behind her seat to pull out the insulated bag.

"Where are we?" Winston asked, looking around.

"We're at Wheaton Park. I thought you'd like it. I'm starved and we can sit at the picnic table and eat." She looked at him curiously. "You can eat right?"

"I have not tried to eat since I have been in the portrait," Winston admitted.

"Well, we'll see what this might bring." Marleigh opened the door, getting out then tossed the insulated bag into Winston's lap. "Here, you carry this and I'll get the portrait."

"Won't we draw attention with me dressed in uniform and you carrying the portrait? I do not want to cause any trouble."

"People should mind their own business," Marleigh replied, dragging the portrait over to a nearby picnic table.

Winston followed dutifully, grabbing his hat and sword. He then sat them down, before placing the bag on the table beside them.

Marleigh opened the bag removing two sandwiches, some chips and two bottles of water.

"I say," Winston said holding up the water. "Did you put water in these bottles? Clever!"

She laughed. "No, I bought the water."

"Why on earth would you purchase water?" Winston asked. "Is there a drought? Even so, I think selling water during a drought would be illegal."

"There is no drought," Marleigh explained as she opened her Ziploc bag with the sandwiches in them. "I like to buy bottled water."

"Why on earth would anyone buy water?" He looked entirely perplexed. "When you can get water for free?"

"Bottled water is supposed to be cleaner and healthier," Marleigh explained.

Winston stared at the bottle. "Then why not just boil your water? That is what we do."

"We don't boil water for drinking, Winston," Marleigh said biting her sandwich.

"You Yanks are strange. Buying water is waste of funds in my opinion." He took a sip after biting into his sandwich and sat down the bottle. "Tastes like any other water."

Marleigh rolled her eyes. "Do you like the ham sandwich?"

"Yes, it is good," Winston said taking a bite. "What are these?"

"Potato chips," she responded.

"I remember these. I saw the ad on the telly once. 'You can't eat just one.'" He took a bite. "A bit salty, but I am sure I could eat just one if I had to." He proceeded to eat the rest of the chips.

"So, did you enjoy your time in the army?" Marleigh asked.

"Yes," Winston replied. "I wanted to get into politics. My father was in the House of Commons and I wanted to follow in his footsteps. More than likely, I did do just that, but I cannot remember since that would have happened years after the portrait was painted."

"I think it's terrible that the witch took away your memory of your later years. What in the world was she thinking?" Marleigh said shaking her head.

"Perhaps she thought I would be pining after my wife and children if I had them," Winston speculated. "All I can remember is my parents and my brother."

"Were you a happy child?" Marleigh asked.

"Yes, for the most part. I was a poor student however, which was a disappointment to my father. I didn't get much attention from him anyway and then he became ill. He died after I graduated and entered into Her Majesty's Service. He had told me countless times that all I could hope to be was a soldier."

"Well, that wasn't very nice," Marleigh pointed out. "Were there other things you liked to do?"

"Oh, I loved to write." Winston looked excited. "While in school, I wrote letters and poetry which were published in the school newspaper. I loved history and that was one area that I did excel in." He picked up his sword and jumped up on the picnic table. "I loved to fence, and I actually won a competition." He waved the sword around. He turned to her and bowed from atop the table. "Since you gave me such a lovely lunch taking me outside, I will recite a poem I wrote. I shall also show you some of my fencing skills against an imaginary opponent."

"Please do," Marleigh said laughing.

Winston bowed to her again, holding his sword above his head. He then slowly bought it down and bent his knees extending his arm that held the sword with the other arm behind his back. "This is called a lunge," he explained while eying her. "Now I will attempt to recite my poem entitled, "My Victory.""

Marleigh had to admit he was too sexy for his own good. The tight uniform kept her mind wandering to places it shouldn't go. His glorious copper mane revealed shades of autumn, red, orange and brown as it now looked somewhat unkempt as he moved gracefully on the table. His muscles bulged as he recited his poem and she found herself glancing at the faint outline of the other bulge. Winston continued to recite and she forced her eyes back on his face. He was a good-looking man even if he was 145 years old.

Suddenly, Winston raised his voice as he continued to recite, slashing the air with his sword for effect.

Marleigh stared up at him entranced, her mouth slack with her heart beating fast. A movement caught her eye and she looked around to see a man with a camera approaching. "Someone's coming," she said standing and putting her hand on Winston's arm to stop him from continuing.

Winston looked up, quickly jumping off the table.

Marleigh had enough sense to turn the portrait around which had been propped against a tree.

"Hello," the man said eying them curiously. "I couldn't help but notice your dancing on the table and your uniform. Are you in a band?" Short and slim with dirty blond hair which peeked out from a faded apple jack cap, he grinned at the two of them. Removing his cap, he turned his focus on Winston.

Marleigh couldn't help but wonder why this man felt he had the right to come over and question them. "No, he's not in a band. Can I help you? What do you want," she snapped. She knew she sounded rude, but something about this joker didn't sit right with her.

Winston quickly bowed, extending his hand. "Winston Spencer at your service."

The man stepped back and looked from Winston to Marleigh, but then took Winston's hand and shook it. He grinned slyly, focusing on Winston. "Oh, I didn't realize you were a foreigner. British right? I can tell by your accent."

"Yes," Winston replied.

"What part of England are you from?" the man asked, turning his back to Marleigh and giving Winston his full attention.

Marleigh didn't like his actions one bit and debated on whether or not to give this fool a piece of her mind.

"Oxfordshire," Winston responded. "And who are you, sir?"

"Oh," the man responded laughing nervously. "I'm Jett Graham from the Daily Post. I saw you two and your dancing on the table with that sword, and I couldn't help but to come over and investigate. I'd love to get a few shots of you in action."

"I was not dancing," Winston replied clearly offended. "I was merely demonstrating some fencing moves."

"Fencing?" Jett Graham replied surprised. "You're holding a sword."

"I used what I had available," Winston countered.

"There's nothing to investigate," Marleigh snapped. "We were minding our own business and not bothering anyone." Moving closer, she crossed her arms and glared at him. He was a few inches shorter than her own five-foot eight frame, and she tried to use her height to intimidate him. "What is the problem?"

"No problem," Jett responded while grinning, seeming to be totally unfazed by her actions. His hazel eyes missed nothing. He returned his focus back to Winston. "Tell me more about your life. Are you here on holiday? What's up with the uniform? I'd love to do a story—"

"I'm sorry, that won't be possible," Marleigh said cutting him off and positioning herself in front of Winston. "Come on Winston, we have to leave." Turning away from Jett Graham, she didn't like the sly smile he wore. The last thing she needed today was some nosy reporter asking questions.

"Of course," Winston responded, blocking Jett Graham's view as she grabbed the portrait. He bowed once again. "Mr. Graham, perhaps another time."

"If you give me your number, I can call you," Jett Graham insisted.

"Uh, I do not have a number," Winston replied, quickly moving behind a nearby tree.

Marleigh rushed to the car as fast as she could. She opened the rear door and pushed the painting inside. She glanced back at the picnic table and saw Jett Graham looking around as if he'd lost something. She'd forgotten that Winston would disappear as soon as she put a few yards of space between them. He now was nowhere around. She knew he was safely back in the portrait, and more than likely, Jett Graham was wondering about what happened to him. She just hoped he hadn't seen Winston disappear right before his very eyes. Why did she think bringing Winston out in public was a good idea? She felt like kicking herself.

She hurriedly got in the car as she saw Jett Graham rushing towards her. She then put the car in gear and sped off.

Chapter Five

WINSTON CURSED UNDER his breath as he found himself back in the portrait once again. Not only that, Marleigh in her haste had placed him in the backseat of her motor car, upside down. He found himself staring at the back of the seat she was sitting in.

He wanted her to call him forth, but knew this would not happen until she had him safely back in her apartment. Things had been going so well until that blighter calling himself a reporter had shown up. For a moment, he'd felt like his old self. He felt free with the sun shining on his face as he'd recited the poem.

Noting how Marleigh's face had been glowing as she'd watched his antics, he had seen something else as well...desire. She wanted him. It had become obvious to him, even if she hadn't yet realized it. Her hungry eyes had wandered over his frame, making him feel even more alive, knowing that they both felt the attraction between them. It made him feel on top of the world, and he wondered how far she would actually take her unacknowledged desires.

This was new territory for both of them, and he was not sure if a relationship would even be possible. Before he knew it, the motor car had stopped and she'd opened the back-passenger door, pulling him out. She kicked the car door shut with her foot and hurried to the apartment as if the hounds of hell were on her heels. When they were safely inside, she sat him down.

She looked as if she was out of breath. Walking over to the large electric ice box, she opened the door removing another bottle of water which she swiftly downed. "Winston, come forth." She set the bottle down while plopping down in a chair and closing her eyes.

"Well that was fun," he stated hoping to calm her nerves.

It didn't work.... in fact, it had the opposite effect.

"Fun?" She stared at him in disbelief, as she jumped to her feet. "We almost got found out! What if he saw you disappear right before his eyes?"

Winston held up his hands defensively and lowered his voice as he spoke, "He did not. I ducked behind a tree when I saw that you were leaving without me. You panicked and abandoned me." He tried to sound hurt and shook his head. He put his arm across his forehead in an act of dismay in an effort to ease her tension with humor. "I am truly traumatized."

"I bet," Marleigh said unimpressed, but she seemed to calm down, and then smiled at him. "I have to admit, that was quick thinking on your part to get out of his direct line of vision."

"A soldier must be able to react quickly." Winston smirked, saluting her. "I am known for my quick wit and being able to outsmart the enemy."

Marleigh rolled her eyes again. "Yeah, right."

"Marleigh, when will we go out again?" Winston asked following her as she picked up the portrait and carried it back to her bedroom.

She sat the portrait on the floor and turned to him. "Again? What makes you think I'll set myself up for another near heart attack?" She shook her head. "That was pure stupidity on my part. We never should have gone out." Heading over to the window, she looked out.

Winston stepped up behind her blocking her in. She turned around and he moved closer, gazing into her large brown eyes. He placed his hand against the wall and leaned down bringing his face close to hers. She smelled like vanilla and reminded him of the fairy cakes his mother used to make from time to time. "It was not stupidity.

Nothing bad happened, and we both had an enjoyable time. We just have to be more careful, that is all."

"Winston," she said ducking under his arm and walking to the bed. "We almost got caught."

"*Almost* is the operative word," he pointed out grinning. "We just have to be more careful and plan things better next time."

"We can't take any further chances," Marleigh said stubbornly.

Winston moved closer, looking determined. Today had been perfect. He felt alive again, and he didn't want to lose it. He had to convince her. "You know you want to take me out again," he insisted. "You like me, I can tell."

"What has that got to do with it?" Marleigh asked while backing up.

"You were not listening to my poem; you were watching me and you were aroused. There is a connection between us. Plus, spending time out of your apartment and my prison gave me hope."

Marleigh appeared stunned and her embarrassment was obvious. "You—you're crazy. There's nothing between us. You're imagining things."

"Am I?" he asked, pulling her into his arms. "So, what I feel for you is all one sided? I was watching you also. I cannot get the picture of you naked from your bath out of my mind. I knew you were watching me too when I was out there on top of that table...and I liked it."

He then bent his head and captured her lips before she could reply.

MARLEIGH HADN'T EXPECTED the rush of pure heat and lust to consume her as Winston held her in his arms, kissing her. She'd never felt like this before. His erection pressed against her belly and she wondered if they could...no! She couldn't think about that. He felt like a real man. He smelled like one too. She wasn't exactly sure what the scent was, but she could smell it and she couldn't deny the attraction she felt. "What is the scent you are wearing?" she whispered.

Winston smiled down at her, his blue-green eyes bright. "Trumper...extract of limes from India. It is my favorite. It is hard to believe that you can smell it since I applied it over a hundred years ago."

Unable to help herself, she placed her arms around his neck and pulled his face down for a kiss. His lips attacked hers hungrily. She felt like a starving woman coming off of a long fast. She wanted him and it was obvious, he wanted her also.

Her hand slid around to his erection and she squeezed it through his tight pants. It was huge and heavy and just the feel of him made her wet. There were buttons on his fly, not a zipper and she couldn't undo them. She squeezed him again.

Groaning, he crushed her body into his own.

He had been wrong in calling her a virgin. She wasn't, but she hadn't been sexually active since her first year of college.... six years ago. She'd been curious and stupid and her then boyfriend had an almost nonexistent libido. Then she'd caught him with another woman, so his libido did exist, just not with her. Immediately, she broke off their relationship.

She unbuttoned Winston's uniform jacket and pushed it down his arms until it fell in the floor. The white shirt he wore underneath was next thing she wanted to remove. She pulled it from his trousers, still kissing him. She wanted him naked and all these clothes were a challenge.

Winston broke the kiss and chuckled. "Slow down, luv," he urged while grabbing her behind, his lips nibbling her ear. His hands slid under her sweater and squeezed her breasts as he claimed her lips once again. Releasing her mouth, he gazed into her eyes.

"What happened to being a gentleman?" she asked breathless from his kisses.

"I am a gentleman," Winston replied, releasing her and backing off. "However, I am still a man." Slowly, he unbuttoned his shirt, his eyes never leaving hers.

"I'm not a virgin," Marleigh murmured as she watched hungrily, missing his warmth. "Things are different now than they were in your day. Virginity is no longer a requirement in order to have a good reputation."

"Ah, well in my day, intercourse was still happening between married as well as the unmarried. However, people tried to be discreet. I gather that much has not changed in modern times." Winston placed his hands behind his back as he stood at ease like the soldier he was.

His torso looked muscled, pale and hard. Marleigh moved in for a closer look. Freckles sprinkled his arms; his nipples were flat and rosy, with a spattering of hair spread across the middle of his chest. The man was absolutely gorgeous—a pale beautiful, living and breathing Michelangelo.

With her eyes wandering lower, she noticed he was still somewhat hard. She wished she hadn't said anything about him being a gentleman. Now he seemed a bit withdrawn. It had been so long for her and even back then, she hadn't felt like this. What harm could it be to explore her options? "What do you want?" she ventured, trying to get him to look at her.

"What do you mean?" Winston asked, looking around but not meeting her eyes.

"Do you want me? Because I want you, Winston. You were right. I was aroused. I'm still aroused...and wet."

His head jerked up at her confession and their eyes locked.

"Am I shocking you?"

He rapidly closed the space between them, grabbing her under her ample bottom and lifting her up. Her legs naturally went around his waist. His restraint was gone, and now she knew nothing would hold him back. "I am not shocked," he responded, his eyes heavy lidded. "I just never thought the day would come where I would hear a woman tell me that her cunt was dripping honey just for me."

"Cunt, huh?" Marleigh laughed. "Yes, my British friend, my honey pot is weeping for what you have there in your pants."

Lust flared in his eyes as he stood at full attention, once again pressing hard into her stomach. He put her down and grabbed the bottom of her sweater, pulling it over her head.

Snatching it from him, she carelessly tossed it over her shoulder.

"Show me everything," he demanded. "I want to see every inch of your skin where you put that moisturizer, when I watched you from the portrait."

"You were watching me," Marleigh stated in surprise.

"Every night," he confessed, tugging at her jeans.

She pushed his hand away and unbuttoned them, pushing them down her legs. Stepping out of them, she heard him inhale as he stared at her purple panties.

"My god! You are going to make me spill before I even get inside you," he confessed.

"Then we will take our time, won't we?" Marleigh giggled, putting her arms around his neck. Just his words, his Victorian speech, and his British accent made her hot and horny. This man would probably drive her to the brink of insanity, but she welcomed it with open arms.

WINSTON HAD NOT EXPECTED this. He had been with women before while in school. He had been careful and always used a johnny or a condom as the Americans called them. He was not about to go the way of his father, but he didn't have a johnny. Did modern women keep such things on hand? His knowledge of modern sexual practices was nonexistent. At one time, he knew what to expect, but that was over one hundred years ago. He did not know this woman, not really. Yet, he wanted her with an intensity he could not explain.

"Show me everything," he demanded in a voice that didn't sound like his own. He watched as she took off her undergarment revealing round breasts with nipples that reminded him of the summer blackberries he loved so much. "You are beautiful," he whispered in awe. "Beautiful enough to drive a man insane."

Smiling, she was apparently pleased at his words.

He felt his heart soar.

There had been very few Negro women in England. In fact, he'd only seen one when he'd went down to Cuba. Never, had he imagined he would have an opportunity like this. He licked his lips in anticipation. Then she pulled down her jeans and he saw her purple knickers. Purple! He stared at her, mesmerized, unable to look away. His cock ached and he took it in hand without even thinking and began to stroke himself.

Slowly, she pulled down the purple garment and then stood before him, gloriously naked.

Her brown skin shone, reminding him of the Queen cakes made with ginger and molasses that his mother would serve on Boxing Day. Why did everything about her remind him of food? Maybe because he was about to taste every delicious part of her. "Beautiful," he growled in appreciation.

She smiled at him. "I guess I won't have to worry about pregnancy."

"I do not think so," he replied. "And hopefully, I do not have to worry about catching any disease from you, since I do not have a johnny or a condom, as you Americans say."

Before he knew what was happening, she took a step forward and slapped his face. "I'm not a whore. I don't have any diseases!"

He touched his stinging cheek as she snatched up her clothes from the floor and walked into the bathroom slamming the door.

Inexplicably and abruptly, Winston found himself back in the portrait, wondering what in the world had just happened.

TREMBLING WITH ANGER, Marleigh stared at her reflection in the mirror. A disease? Why did he have to ruin the mood with that comment?

When Winston spoke about not catching anything from her, she'd seen red and had slapped him without hesitation. How could he say such a thing? Did he think that she had a disease because she hadn't played hard to get?

As soon as she'd seen the shocked look on his face, she remembered that this man came from another time. A time when women remained virgins until marriage unless they were in a committed relationship or were in fact... whores. Maybe she'd overreacted, but his question had hurt her.

She hurriedly washed her face and straightened her stance. Hind sight was twenty-twenty and the truth was they had moved too quickly. Maybe it was a good thing this had happened before they'd done something they would later regret. After all, what had come over her? How could there ever be a chance of a real relationship with this man. He wasn't a real man, was he? He was some sort of ghost who had been locked in a portrait; a man who would remain 21 even after she became an old woman. She needed to get her head on straight.

Putting her clothes back on, she came out of the bathroom. She realized Winston was back in the portrait and she refused to look at him. She couldn't call him forth because she needed some time to figure things out.

Tugging her shoes on, Marleigh grabbed her purse and walked out of the room. Needing some air and a few minutes to clear her head, she left the apartment.

Chapter Six

MARLEIGH DROVE TO THE Food Lion, not far from her home and picked up a few things.

Needing to return to work the next day, she knew she should clear the air with Winston. After thinking about their conversation, she realized maybe Winston's concern could've been based on his own life experiences. One hundred years ago, there was no cure for diseases like syphilis and men had to be careful or pay the price.

She sighed and rushed through the checkout. As she was heading to her car, she heard someone yelling and she quickly looked behind her.

"Ma'am excuse me!" Jett Graham was heading her way. He wore the same apple jack cap with a well-worn tee shirt and jeans.

Groaning, she pushed her cart to the trunk of her car, and raised it.

"I'm surprised to run into you again," he said grinning like a Cheshire cat as he approached her. "Where's your friend?"

"I'm sure he's somewhere taking care of his own business," Marleigh replied, trying to remain calm.

"Really," Jett said looking around. "Why don't you give me his full name and number? As I recall, he told me that he didn't have a number, but he said that his name was Winston Spencer, and then he just disappeared. It was all so cloak and dagger and now, I wonder if he's here illegally? You wouldn't know anything about that, would you?"

Marleigh gave him a hard stare. "How would I know that? I just met him myself!"

"Is that so," Jett responded in disbelief, looking as if he had suspicions of some kind. "You know some foreigners prey on the sympathies of well-meaning Americans and try to insert themselves in their lives. They fraudulently seek to get green cards by sweeping unsuspecting women off their feet and marrying them. I've been working on a piece for my paper."

Marleigh slammed the trunk. The paper he worked for was no better than a tabloid, and she wasn't about to give him any information. She turned to Jett, barely able to remain civil. "So, you think that I'm some dumb unsuspecting woman," she asked, glaring at him.

"I'm just saying that you two were acting very suspicious when I mentioned that I was a reporter and wanted to do a piece on your friend. It had me thinking that maybe he's not on the up and up."

"Maybe he's just a private person," Marleigh snapped. "Not everyone wants to be on the front page as news."

"Did he tell you why he was in the country?" Jett pressed. "Why was he dressed in that uniform? What was he up to?"

"You know," Marleigh replied while opening the driver side door. "I didn't ask him. We were just enjoying each other's company. Now if you will excuse me, I have to leave."

Jett backed up as she got in the car and started the engine. He tapped on the window.

With a grunt, she lowered it a bit.

"Here's my card," he insisted. "Have your friend call me."

"Right," Marleigh said narrowing her eyes while tossing the card onto the passenger seat. Pulling away, she watched Jett get into a blue pickup truck as she glanced in her rear-view mirror. She had driven about a mile and noticed he was following her. She wasn't about to lead him to her apartment, so she headed to her parent's home instead.

Pulling up in the driveway, she felt thankful her old house key was still on the ring. Exiting the car, she walked up to the door and opened it with the key, hoping he would think she lived here. She rushed in and shut the door, peeking out the window.

Sure enough, Jett had parked across the street. He sat there for a few moments and then left.

"Well, this is a surprise!"

Marleigh turned around and saw her mother standing in the doorway. "A reporter was following me, and I didn't want to go home," she explained.

Her mother's eyes widened. "What on earth? Why was he following you?"

"I was talking to this guy, he was from Britain and this reporter, Jett Graham just came over and inserted himself in the conversation. I blew him off and then today, I went to the Food Lion near my apartment, and there he was. He was spouting nonsense about foreigners being in the country illegally and wanted to interview me because he knew that some were taking advantage of women to remain here in the country."

"Wow," her mother said shaking her head. "And he got all that from watching you talk to this young man?"

"It was crazy." Marleigh groaned, shaking her head in disbelief.

"So where is this young man now?" her mother asked curiously.

"I believe he's gone back to where he stays," Marleigh replied evasively. "That guy Jett wants to interview him to see if he's really here legally. Can you believe that?"

Her mother shook her head. "Well, with the climate in this country right now, I wouldn't be surprised at anything. Come on. I'll fix you some lunch."

"No, mom. I have food in the car. I should get it home," Marleigh insisted.

"Very well," her mother replied. "Then come for dinner tonight."

"Tomorrow would be better," Marleigh said, knowing that refusing would only lead to more questions from her mother. "I'll come as soon as I get off work."

"Great," her mother responded. "I'll see you then."

WINSTON STARED AROUND the empty room, wondering when she would return. He had obviously upset her. He realized this now. He had voiced his fears because he didn't have a bloody johnny and because of that, he had hurt her feelings. He knew he needed to explain himself. He doubted now, if he would ever get to leave this room again any time soon. He figured he would have to hold onto the memory of his wonderful afternoon of sightseeing and going to the park. The sun was setting and the light in the room began to dim.

He heard the key in the lock and his heart jumped. She had returned and he hoped she would allow him to apologize for his behavior.

He watched her every move.

Entering the bedroom, she kicked off her shoes. She closed the blinds and turned on the light on the nightstand. She then sat on the bed and stared at him, not saying anything. Suddenly she stood and walked out of the room.

His previous hopes were dashed to the ground. Maybe she needed more time before she felt like talking to him.

Coming back in the room, she looked directly at him. "Winston, come forth," she said firmly.

"I am ever so sorry for offending you, Marleigh," he spoke as soon as he could. He kept his distance and watched her.

Sighing, she sat down on the bed. "I know you weren't trying to offend me," Marleigh replied folding her hands in her lap and staring at them. "But it made me realize that maybe we were moving too quickly. We need to talk more, learn more about each other. There are cures now for a lot of diseases that killed people in your time. Then again, there are some diseases we still don't have cures for." She looked up from her hands and their eyes locked. "We need to proceed with caution, and not rush into anything. Sex can wait, at least for a while. We don't even know the consequences of such behavior. Perhaps you need to consult those rules you said that Temperance the witch told you about."

"The diary is probably still in Miles daughter's possession unless she sold it," Winston surmised. "Perhaps you can go back to her and purchase it and see what it says. Sex was something that hadn't been discussed when Temperance told me the rules, and I was not even thinking along those lines when she owned me." He shivered in disgust at the thought.

"Perhaps I will," Marleigh agreed.

Winston took her hand in his. "You still look upset. What is wrong?"

"That reporter Jett showed up and followed me when I was out. I don't think we can go back out any time soon."

"What did he want?" Winston asked surprised.

"He wants to find out if you're in the country illegally. Can you believe it? He's doing some story and wants to talk to you. We have to be careful."

Winston reluctantly agreed with her, as much as he wanted to go out again. "I think my uniform makes me stick out. I wish I had other clothes."

"I can get you some," Marleigh said now looking excited. "I just have to figure out your size. We can't go far, but maybe you can at least go outside for a short period."

Winston quickly wrote his sizes on a piece of paper on the nightstand and handed it to her. "So, let's talk," he said walking over to the bed and patting it. "You said we need to get to know each other better. What do you want to know?"

Marleigh sat down beside him.

He sat his furry hat down on the floor.

"I love your hair," she said grinning. "The color of it is so unique. Some coppery red and some reddish brown, then some parts are lighter than the others. When the light hits it...I can't stop staring."

Winston laughed. "Well, I am... *was* the only red-haired person in my family. It has toned down a bit since I was a young boy. At one point, it was particularly bright and with my fair skin and freckles, I was a sight."

Marleigh laughed and patted his hand. "I think you're handsome."

"Do you now?" he asked grinning, his confidence building.

"I do," she replied leaning forward and kissing him.

Winston groaned. "We have got to behave...at least for a while."

"Yes." Marleigh sighed.

Winston still thought they needed to clear the air about what had upset her earlier. "I am ever so sorry. I wasn't suggesting that you had a disease. It is just that my father was a bit of a cad, and he got sick...you know...he caught something. It was syphilis. There was no cure and he eventually died."

Marleigh nodded. "I know that there was no cure in your day, but there is now. Still, no one wants to get it. I now understand why you asked. I've only had one man in my bed."

Winston looked surprised. "Really? Was it a bad departure?"

"Not really," Marleigh said staring down at her hands. "I caught him cheating and that was the end of us as far as I was concerned."

"You mean he was with another? He was a damn fool," Winston declared, taking her hand.

"What about you?" she asked.

"I and some of my mates used to leave University and go out on weekends. Sometimes, I would meet up with a girl. Most of them I did not actually have intercourse with...some just wanted company. There were only two and I made sure that I used a johnny...uh I mean condom."

"Well, that was smart. We should take it slow. You don't have to go back in the painting. Stay here in the bed with me, sleep only...no funny business."

Her request startled him. Could he actually lie beside her while she slept? He hadn't slept in years and he didn't seem to need sleep. Still, the request was tempting and he wanted to try it. "Of course," he responded, feeling enthused. Never, in his wildest dreams, had he thought he would be able to lie in a bed again. He realized suddenly, with Marleigh, he could once again experience many of the things from his past that people took for granted, and he was very grateful.

With a smile, she grabbed a gown from the chest of drawers and walked into the bathroom shutting the door.

Moments later, he was back in the painting again, but he knew it wouldn't be for long. Soon, he would actually be lying next to Marleigh.

Chapter Seven

MARLEIGH TRIED TO TAMP down the lust raging through her. The scent of the lime cologne he wore intensified when Winston removed his coat.

She watched as he folded it and placed it on the chair. Then he removed his shirt and she noticed how the hair there was fairer than the hair on his head. Their eyes met, and she felt her sex throb. Who did she think she was fooling? She wanted him, not just for a sleeping partner. She'd been the one who'd said they shouldn't rush into sex, yet this was exactly what she wanted.

Winston came and sat on the side of the bed next to her, removing his boots and socks. He then turned and stood before her as his eyes met hers, his questioning stare unnerving.

Marleigh became acutely aware that she was in fact, sending him mixed signals.

He then slowly unbuttoned his pants; his erection already straining against his trousers. He paused and turned away from her.

"Please don't," she pleaded.

He turned back around to face her and smiled.

Marleigh wondered if this was how men responded when they watched strippers; because her whole body felt on fire, her eyes were glued to his fingers as he undid the last button.

He pulled down the trousers and stepped out of them, his eyes never leaving hers.

She realized now that she'd been holding her breath, and felt a little dizzy. Then her focus shifted to his unusual underpants. She'd never seen anything like them. They were white cotton, of course, but they had a waistband of about five inches without any elastic, with three large white buttons on the front that secured them. The legs of the underpants fit his legs loosely and extended to his knees. Strings dangled on the outside of each of the legs of the garment.

Walking over to the chair with his folded pants, he placed them on top of the other garments seeming to be in no particular hurry. Turning, he moved back over to the bed. The cotton underwear looked thin and left little to the imagination. The fly was tented from his semi hard cock, straining to be free.

She felt a tinge of disappointment as he covered it with his hands, climbed into the bed and under the covers. He lay on his side holding up his head, facing her while grinning. "Say something," He chuckled.

"I've never seen underwear like you're wearing," was all she could think of. Her mouth had become dry, he smelled like pure heaven, and she wondered why the hell she'd even suggested this arrangement. No way would she be getting any sleep. What she really wanted was to see everything he had, but she wasn't about to go there.

"Ah, well I guess times have changed," Winston responded, turning on his back with his hands under his head, staring at the ceiling. "as well as men's small clothes."

"Small clothes?"

"Yes, what you just called underwear; I know as small clothes."

"Is this as hard for you as it is for me?" Marleigh murmured. "I don't know how much sleep I'll get."

"This was your idea, remember?" Winston pointed out.

"I know," Marleigh admitted. She turned her back to him and felt his arms go around her, pulling her closer.

"You just let me know what you want," he said kissing her shoulder. "I will not rush you...ever."

Marleigh turned over and looked into his blue green eyes, closing her own and inhaling. She felt weak, needy and hot. She ran her fingers over his chest, rubbing the coarse hair she found there. She kissed his lips, tentatively at first, and then found herself on top of him as he took control.

She grinned down at him. "You know you're tempting me to jump your bones," she said kissing him.

"Jump my bones?" Winston exclaimed. "How odd...yet how appropriately stated."

"So what did you call it in your day?" Marleigh asked, pressing her stomach against the erection she felt.

"Amorous congress," Winston replied. "And this," he said as he palmed her backside. "Was called, *Playing at St. George*...you know...you being on top. Also, there is the *beast with two backs.*"

Marleigh laughed. "Now, I've heard that one somewhere...maybe in an old movie." Her smile faded a bit. "Winston...I'm sorry. I shouldn't be arousing you. That's not fair."

Winston stared up at her. "Pay no attention to the man behind the curtain. I will not go further than you want me to."

Marleigh laughed. "What do you know about The Wizard of Oz?"

"It was one of Miles' favorites," Winston said. "He had a plastic copy of it that he used to play from time to time."

"You mean video?"

"Yes, a video," Winston nodded.

She slid off of him. "Now, I'm going to sleep. I have to go to work in the morning. I'll be home late because I'm having dinner with my parents."

Winston pouted. "Without me?"

"Well, I can't very well lug the painting over there, now can I?"

"No, that would certainly bring up questions," Winston sighed.

Marley leaned over and kissed him. "Goodnight, Winston."

WINSTON FOUND HIMSELF back in the painting sooner than he'd realized. Marleigh had gotten up to relive herself and he was back, fully dressed as soon as she shut the bathroom door. He sighed thinking it had been good while it lasted. He watched as she walked out of the bathroom half asleep and climbed back into bed. In a few moments, he could hear her snore and knew that most likely, she wouldn't wake up again until it was time for her to do so.

He certainly had enjoyed his time lying beside her, holding her, kissing her. It made him feel like a man once again and not a ghost. He had held her in his arms and felt her breath on his face as she slept. It was glorious and he realized the small things he'd taken for granted before he had become trapped in the painting.

Having the sun on your face, smelling the grass, walking back and forth. All those things he had done before, without a second thought. Now, he cherished the memory of the day he had spent with Marleigh.

He thought about the poem he wrote. He was determined have victory again. Maybe the answer was in Temperance's diary. The thought of once again, being able to fence, to make love to a woman, to be able to live. He also realized in order for that to happen, Marleigh was the only one who could make it possible.

MARLEIGH SAT AT HER parent's home and tried not to think about Winston being all alone. What did she have to feel guilty about? He'd been alone for years. She'd tried to make things better by hanging him on the wall and turning on the television in her bedroom to the cable news channel where he had a direct view.

She'd been surprised to find him gone when she'd awakened that morning and had quickly called him forth, wondering why he'd disappeared. He'd quickly explained what had happened, and cut her off when she tried to apologize.

He liked the idea of leaving the television on while she was away and assured her that he would be fine.

Her day at work had been busy and she felt glad the time had flown by. Now she sat in the living room with her father. Her mother had chased her out of the kitchen, stating that dinner would be ready shortly.

"So did you hang that soldier on the wall in your bare living room," her father asked sipping his beer. "I told Fred that I couldn't believe you'd actually bought that thing in a yard sale. Your uncle then casually told me that it was better than a real White boy being in your apartment, and I had to agree with him."

"Uncle Fred told me what you said." Marleigh laughed. "What's wrong with White boys and what do you have against my portrait?"

"Nothing," Her father replied with a shrug. "I was just messing with you. I don't hold nothing against anyone that treats you right. You remember that! I've met plenty of assholes of all colors."

"Amen!" her mother said walking into the living room. "Let's eat."

Just then, the doorbell rang.

"Who could that be?" her father said getting up. "I hope it's not someone selling something." He opened the door.

Marleigh was shocked to see Jett Graham standing there. The nerve of the man.

"Good evening," Jett said trying to look over her father's shoulder.

"May I help you?" Harvey Winters asked in a stern voice.

"My name is Jett Graham and I'm a reporter for the Daily Post. I met a young lady who apparently lives here and I wanted to do a story."

"And I told you that I wasn't interested," Marleigh said walking up to the door.

"Marleigh, what's this about?" her father asked looking over at her.

"You see sir," Jett said before she could reply. "I happened to see this young lady out in the park the other day with a young British man dressed in a uniform. They seemed to be enjoying the day and he was on top of the table jumping around, waving a sword as if he were fencing."

"What?" Her father looked startled. "Fencing?" He turned to Marleigh. "What's he talking about?"

"Daddy, I was just talking to a young man and for some reason, this fool thinks that he's an illegal alien or something."

Just then, she noticed her mother listening in the doorway.

"Is this the man that was following you...stalking you the other day," she asked as she walked over to them.

"I was not stalking anybody," Jett said defensively. "I was only trying to get information for my story."

"Now, you listen boy," her father said sternly. "Don't make me have to go to the police. You shouldn't be stalking my daughter. If she says she's not interested in giving you a story, you need to find someone else to write about. Don't make me have to file a complaint with that paper you work for."

Jett drew himself up. "Well, I beg your pardon. I thought your daughter was of age to make her own decisions."

"I am," Marleigh replied. "And I've told you that I'm not interested."

"What about Winston, your friend. I want him to tell me to my face, he's not interested. Where is he?"

Marleigh grabbed the door. "We're about to have dinner. You need to go!" She then quickly slammed it in Jett's face and turned to her parents. "Let's eat."

"HOW WAS DINNER?" WINSTON asked when she came home and freed him from his portrait prison.

Marleigh sat on the bed and fell backwards staring at the ceiling. "Jett Graham showed up at my parent's house! He's such a persistent ass!"

"What did you tell him?" Winston asked removing his sword and hat.

Marleigh sat up and watched as he sat in the chair and removed his boots and socks. "I told him that I wasn't interested in doing a story and he had the nerve to tell me that he wouldn't take 'no' for an answer unless you told him so, face to face."

Winston laughed and then sat beside her. "Well that won't happen, will it."

"Of course, his meddling had my parents asking questions about you over dinner." Marleigh groaned. "I told them that you were someone I just happened to meet and that I didn't even know your address or phone number, which wasn't a lie. I just wish Jett Graham would leave us alone!"

He leaned over and kissed her. "Do not worry about it. He will grow tired of trying to change your mind and most likely, will find someone else to pester."

"I hope so. Did you learn anything today from the news show I left on the television?"

"Yes, our Prime Minister is a woman!" Winston exclaimed. "Can you believe that? I was shocked!"

Marleigh laughed. "So, you don't think a woman would be good in politics? There are lots of women in politics now, Winston. Besides, Queen Elizabeth is your sovereign now like Victoria was your Sovereign, back in your day."

Shaking his head, he removed his coat and folded it on the chair. "Yes, well I know the current Queen is the great-great granddaughter. From what I can tell, she is doing a bang-up job. It is just strange watching the telly and seeing so many changes that have occurred over the years." He turned and noticed her hungry look as she stared at his bare chest.

Standing before her, he slowly began unbuttoning his pants, his eyes never leaving hers. He saw her ample breasts move with her breathing as she watched him. He knew he was tempting her. She had won the battle last night, but he had a feeling that tonight... she would be his.

"You're sure of yourself, aren't you," she whispered, trying to sound confident and failing miserably.

"Not when it comes to you," he replied. He let the pants drop and stepped out of them. He was about to turn to pick up his pants when she grabbed his hand. He glanced down at her hand against his pale skin and slowly looked back up to her.

She let go of his wrist and before he realized what she was doing, she freed his cock from the confines of his drawers.

He stared down at it in her soft brown hands, holding him. For the first time he noticed her nails were painted in an aqua color.

She squeezed him and licked her lips. Then she leaned forward and licked the purple head.

He could not contain the groan in his throat. "You should not..." he weakly protested.

She did not listen as she engulfed him in her mouth and slid down his length.

His body trembled at such a glorious feeling, one that he'd never experienced before. At that moment, he could deny her nothing.

She used her other hand to gently massage his cods and her tongue swirled around the sensitive head before sliding down his length once again. She kept sucking and sucking as he threw his head back in ecstasy. He found his hand in her hair and he was squeezing because he was so near to completion.

He had heard of this act; his friends had said that only the lowest of women would perform it... which is why they would have to take a mistress. Wives didn't do such a thing because to do so was to expect reciprocation, and his friends had told him that real men didn't eat cunt. It was all a damnable lie! He knew this now as Marleigh worshiped his cock with her mouth that he longed to taste her also, and he would taste her!

Pulling back, he heard the pop of her luscious lips as he exited her mouth. Breathing hard, he backed up a bit. "I do not wish to spill in your sweet mouth just yet. Take off your clothes and show me your cunny."

"My what?" Marleigh laughed.

"Your little honey pot," Winston said seriously. "I want to see it, NOW!" He barked it as if giving her an order and for a moment, he wondered if she was offended.

She grinned at him as she quickly removed her clothes.

Suddenly, he felt as if he was having a déjà vu moment. He had made a mistake before, but he would be damned if he would make the same mistake twice. "Get on the bed and spread your legs," he commanded. He watched as she complied. "Now," he said as he moved closer, stroking himself. "Take your fingers and show me."

His hand stilled his stroking as she used her fingers to spread her sex. The sight of her sweet skin was almost more than he could bear standing, so he fell to his knees, grabbed her legs, and pulled her to the edge of the bed. He leaned forward and though he'd never done it before, he allowed his instincts to guide him. He ran his tongue along her slit and she tasted salty sweet. His friends had been fools! They did not know what they'd been missing.

He could feel her tense under him and instinctively knew he was missing something. He raised his head. "I have never done this before; you have to instruct me."

"Lick my clit, the little pearl at the top of my slit," she said sounding a bit breathless. "Softly at first...and as I become more aroused, harder."

He dipped his head, his eyes falling on the sensitive bud she spoke about. He closed his eyes so he could concentrate and felt it tremble under his tongue. He heard her groan in approval and her body responded with more wetness, so he knew he was on the right track. The more he licked, the wetter she got, and the harder his cock became.

He didn't think he'd ever tire of doing this, cunnilingus as it was called. It came from the Latin *cunnus* meaning vulva and *lingus* meaning licking. Glorious sweetness was what he called it.

"Oh God, Winston, I'm coming!" Marleigh gasped, as she stiffened under him. He held her tightly as he felt her spasms on his tongue and then she fell back on the bed and began to pull away. He released her and reclined on the bed beside her as he continued to stroke himself.

"That was absolutely..."

"Spectacular," he finished for her.

"Yes," she replied grinning at him.

"And it was my very first time," Winston pointed out. "I try to be a good student when learning new things that interest me."

Marleigh laughed. "You're such a braggart."

"So I have been told," Winston agreed with a grin.

Chapter Eight

MARLEIGH GROANED AT her own total lack of self-control. What was wrong with her? She knew that having Winston in her bed would lead to this! Her mouth said one thing, but her body had its own ideas.

The problem was that this thing between them couldn't be controlled, at least not by her. All of her talk of waiting went out the window the minute she saw him unbuttoning his pants. No, it had been the night before when she'd perused him in his unusual underpants. She'd held it together then, but tonight she couldn't...no she wouldn't deny herself, and she had no regrets.

She now noticed Winston had stopped stroking himself and was watching her. He lay on his side, facing her with his head propped up by his hand.

"Are you all right?" he asked, looking concerned.

"Of course not." She sighed. "I was just thinking that the restraint I spoke about, went out the window. And I couldn't help it. It all made sense when I said it before, but for some reason, I just couldn't wait any longer." She looked down and noticed he still looked hard, though he seemed to be totally calm. "How can you be fine when I haven't finished the job?" she asked taking him in her hand. "Most men would have jumped on top of me as soon as they knew that I'd been satisfied."

Winston chuckled. "I am not most men...at least I'm no longer like most men. I know that I cannot do anything unless I am sure it is what you want. It is part of the spell, I guess. His eyes met hers. "If you say no, the desire for whatever I want leaves me. If you say yes, then my desire increases and I long to please you. It is like you are in total control. My feelings and desires are heightened when you are happy. When you want me, I want you too. I am drawn to you, Marleigh. I cannot explain it exactly. With Temperance, it was never sexual because that's not what she wanted from me. She was a lonely old woman who wanted attention that she couldn't get from her son. She needed someone to talk to, so I provided that. With Miles, he wanted a son because he only had a daughter, so I provided what he wanted. It's like my existence is centered around the desires of my owner and are not my own."

"So, you knew that I wanted you," Marleigh stated.

"Yes," he said closing his eyes as she took his length in her hand and began to stroke him. "Just like I can feel that you want me right now. Your desire draws me, but I want you too and pleasing you, pleases me."

"I do want you," Marleigh admitted, kissing him. "But I want you to be satisfied also."

"I will be when you are," Winston responded. "You care for me and that makes me happy. It makes my prison bearable. The kindness you showed me by taking me outside, caring about my happiness, something that no one has ever done since I have been under this spell, has made me love you."

"What?" Marleigh exclaimed sitting up. "You can't love me."

"But I do," Winston insisted. "Temperance once told me that if I ever found someone who saw me as a real man, something other than just a portrait, someone who cared for me, that I might be able to escape the portrait. She doubted however, that it would ever happen."

"Does that mean there's a way that you'll be able to leave the portrait?" Marleigh asked.

"I do not know," Winston said shaking his head. "She was always closed mouth about it. If I asked too many questions, she would leave the room and I ended up back in the portrait." He grabbed Marleigh's hand. "If you really want to know, you will have to go back to Gertrude's house and see if she has that diary."

Marleigh's head was swimming. Was there a way to free Winston? With Jett Graham hanging around, there was no use in freeing him, only for Winston to end up being deported because he had no papers. She had to think and form a plan. "I will check with Gertrude, but in the meantime, we have to be very careful, Winston."

He put his arms around her and pulled her close, resting his chin on her shoulder as she stared at his portrait. "Of course," he murmured, kissing her shoulder. "Even if it never happens, I want you to know that I never dreamed that things would be this good for me."

Marleigh sighed and turned in his arms. "You love me now because of the spell. I don't want to get my hopes up that you will feel the same way if I find a way to free you."

"I doubt my feelings will change," Winston insisted. "Spell or no spell, I love you Marleigh. Yes, even though you may not realize it, I think that somehow, you have put a crack in the power of that spell. I felt lighter when you took me outside. I felt the heaviness that I normally feel dissipate when you showed me your city. It was as if your kindness to me has somehow weakened the spell. Even when you left me to go to your job, my prison didn't feel so bleak. I cannot explain it."

She shook her head. "Let's just take it one step at a time. I'm going to try to get that diary and maybe we can figure this out."

"Of course," he responded.

Her gaze wandered over his naked frame and she slid closer to him. His hair looked mussed and this k just made him look even sexier. "Now my desire is to finish what we started earlier," she pointed out, pushing him back on the bed.

"I would like that." He chuckled, pulling her closer. "Very much."

She relaxed in his arms as he kissed her. Marleigh accepted his tongue, the kiss heating her whole body in a furnace of pure bliss. She felt his fingers enter her, stroking and caressing. She realized he was still making this about her. No, he wasn't a normal man, he was a saint. She drenched his fingers and felt her release building. Never, had she been aroused with any man like she was with Winston.

This was nothing like her previous experience. She'd enjoyed sex somewhat, but it hadn't been earth shattering. Now she was about to explode again, but she didn't want to fall over the edge into pure bliss without him. "I want you inside me," she said breathlessly staring into his sea blue eyes and stilling his questing fingers. "I want to feel you."

"As you wish," he murmured, grabbing her under her hips as he poised himself at her entrance.

Such a glorious feeling, with him stretching her and filling her. It did feel slightly painful as he pushed himself to possess her fully, but she didn't care. She willed her body to adjust to him. She didn't want him to hold anything back, that would be the last thing she wanted him to do. She clutched his shoulders and wound her legs around him. His eyes were closed as she felt his fingers dig into her backside. She reached up and touched his face.

He opened his eyes.

"What are you thinking?" she asked.

"Thinking..." he gasped as he slammed into her harder. "I...cannot think. I can only feel."

"Then take it all," she insisted. "Feel all of me."

Something seemed to snap in him and he raised her a few inches from the bed as he continued to stroke her hard and fast, his hands gripping her by her buttocks.

"Everything, give me everything you got Winston." Marleigh was coming again, and when she felt his hands tighten painfully on her behind, she knew he was close to coming also.

"*Meus es tu*," he cried as his body stiffened.

Marleigh quickly followed, her body exploding with multiple spasms that started in her center and spread throughout her body.

Her body felt like rubber; her limbs like lead, and every part of her tingled. She hadn't known it could be like this. Was it real or was this just a byproduct of Temperance's spell?

It took tremendous effort, but she turned her head slowly to look over at him.

Winston watched her, as she lay sprawled on her back, totally spent. *"Meus es tu."* he said again, climbing back on top of her, slipping inside her once again.

How could he be ready again so soon? She was sure she would be sore in the morning, but just now, she didn't care. His hard length once again filled her.

"I love you," he whispered as he began slowly thrusting inside her. "I love you, Marleigh...always from this point forward."

She couldn't speak as she felt him move in and out of her. He looked down to where they were joined. "You wanted this between us, and as long as you want me, you will have me. I will fill you, pleasure you, make your body sing."

Marleigh reached up and he leaned closer. She ran her fingers through his hair as it now fell into his eyes. She pushed it back and he grinned down at her.

"But is it real?" she asked. "I mean, suppose it's only this way now because of the spell?"

He didn't answer her, but began to pump in and out of her harder.

Now, she felt herself lose all concept of time. Was she losing her mind because the pleasure was so sweet, so divine, that nothing else mattered for the moment? She came hard for a third time, yet he continued to move, as the rollercoaster feelings were building inside her once again. Pleasure coursed throughout her body as she convulsed when another orgasm consumed her. She thought he'd never stop pumping, but then he cried out as he slammed into her, his own body stiffening, his seed flooding her as he nipped her shoulder before collapsing on the bed.

"What did you say to me earlier?" Marleigh asked quietly. "You spoke in another language."

Winston pulled the covers over the both of them and reached for the light on the nightstand, cutting it off.

The room went dark, but she could feel his breath on her as he pulled her into his arms.

"*Meus es tu,*" he whispered. "It is Latin meaning, 'You are mine.' The thought of you being with someone else is unbearable."

"I'm not with anyone else, I'm with you," Marleigh reassured him. "How do you say, 'always' in Latin?"

"*Semper,*" he responded, kissing her.

"Then...*meus es tu, semper,*" Marleigh whispered, returning his kisses.

Chapter Nine

MARLEIGH SLEEPILY OPENED her eyes and found Winston watching her. "Did you sleep at all?" she asked as she stretched. Her body felt sore, but deliciously so.

"I do not sleep," Winston responded. "However, I enjoyed watching you sleep."

"I see," Marleigh said sitting up. "Apparently, you wore me out because I didn't get up during the night, and now my bladder feels as if it's about to burst."

Winston laughed as she quickly got up and ran into the bathroom.

When she came out, the room was empty and there were no clothes on the chair. She knew he was back in the portrait, fully dressed.

"Winston, come forth," she said grinning. She turned around and found him leaning on the bed post. "I wish I could dress that quickly," she joked, walking up to him and giving him a kiss. "Now I have to shower and get ready for work." She walked over to the television and picked up the remote. "I now have access to BBC News, so I'll leave that on for you to watch while I'm gone," she said setting down the remote.

"Thank you," Winston replied, standing at attention and saluting her. "You should get ready. You do not want to be late for work."

Marleigh laughed as she went into the bathroom and shut the door.

She showered and came out of the room with just a towel. She stopped in front of the portrait remembering the first time she'd stood before the portrait naked. She turned and faced it, and let the towel drop to the floor, grinning seductively. His eyes seemed to burn into her. She sat on the bed and faced him as she lotioned her body, starting with her toes and working her way up. Marleigh got up and faced the portrait then turned her back to him to rub some lotion on her backside. She stretched her arms above her head and then bending over, she touched her toes with her legs spread apart. She turned around and faced the portrait, his stony stare only arousing her more. What was wrong with her? If she kept this up, she would be late for work, but a part of her didn't give a damn. "Winston, come forth," she said firmly, looking at the portrait.

He stood there and for the first time, she actually saw him materialize, his sword strapped to his side, his furry hat on, his pants obviously tented with his erection.

"Marleigh, you have to be to work in forty-five minutes," he pointed out, his voice husky. "You need to get dressed."

"Do I?" she asked sounding innocent. She walked over to him and touched his erection. The sound of the television became background noise.

He kissed her as he picked her up as if she were as light as a feather and dropped her on the bed. He quickly removed his hat and sword, his eyes never leaving her. He then yanked his coat over his head without unbuttoning it completely as he usually did, and she heard a button pop off and hit the floor. He yanked his pants and underwear down, he still wore his boots, his erection pointing at her deliciously.

Marleigh quickly scrambled to her knees and grasped him in her hand.

"Marleigh you are going to be late," he protested.

She ignored him and took him in her mouth, sliding down his length. She would get a small note of infraction for being late, but then again, she'd never been late and she could afford it just this once.

Winston no longer protested, but moved in her mouth with short quick strokes. She felt herself grow wetter and wetter, knowing she would be needing another shower when this was over.

She felt him stiffen and he came like a flood, a glorious salty sweet flood of pure male energy. She swallowed every drop as she looked up at him and saw him smiling with his eyes closed.

He slowly opened his eyes and pulled away from her.

Relaxing back on the bed, she realized that in the few seconds she'd glanced away from his cock, he was hard again...just as hard as he had been before.

"You know you are about to get stuffed," he growled.

Marleigh laughed nervously at his British slang. She knew she had done it now, and she could only hope that she'd make it to work today or she would get docked for a day's pay.

WINSTON LAY ON THE bed as Marleigh scrambled to her feet, eyeing the clock. He had made love to her two more times and noticed how she was not moving as quickly as she normally did. Did he do that? He smiled to himself.

"Damn, I'm late!" she exclaimed grabbing the towel from the floor and groaning as she stretched her muscles. She hurried into the bathroom.

Winston immediately found himself back in the portrait, fully dressed.

He watched the BBC channel and could hear the water from her shower.

She came out of the bathroom wearing only her black cap she slept in.

He watched her, as she swiftly got dressed. She didn't call him forth again and he could understand why, but that didn't stop him from enjoying the view.

He tried to remember all of the rules that Temperance had told him years ago, but at the time, he had been entirely focused on a way to get out of the portrait and not on a relationship. He could tell, however, that something had changed since he'd been in Marleigh's possession.

There had always been a heaviness inside of him and feelings of despair, but now he felt light as a feather. Things weren't as gloomy and he always felt excited to see her, something he'd never experienced with Temperance or Miles. He had never felt this close to either of them, yet it was more than the physical relationship he and Marleigh shared. He couldn't explain it. He could only hope Marleigh would be able to get that diary. Winston knew that it had been in Miles possession.

"I'll see you later," Marleigh said blowing him a kiss. She picked up her purse and left the room.

He heard her shut the front door and her key turning in the lock.

Later, as he was watching the BBC talk about the resignation of Teresa May as the Prime Minister, he heard a key in the front lock and wondered why Marleigh was home early.

He felt shocked to hear men's voices coming from the front of the apartment. Was Marleigh's home being robbed? He heard the men laughing.

"I hear the TV," one of the men said. "Hello? Is anyone home?"

"She must have left it on," another man said. "We'll cut it off when we go in there."

Winston watched helplessly as a man entered the bedroom carrying a can with a nozzle and began to spray a liquid in the corners of the room. He picked up the remote and cut off the television.

"Nope. No one's here, Jerry," he said looking around. His eyes fell on Winston and he laughed. "The girl must like soldiers."

"What?" the other man said walking into the room. He glanced at the portrait and shook his head. "Really man, we don't have time to mess around. We have a lot of apartments to finish fumigating. I didn't see any bugs here, but I think we covered things pretty well. Let's go."

The other man gave Winston one last look, before they both left the room. Winston heard them leave the apartment and replace the lock. He didn't understand what the men were doing, but he was sure that Marleigh would explain. He was glad that she'd at least made the bed before she left, because he didn't like the idea of other men being in her bedroom. He sighed to himself. With no telly to watch, he just had to wait patiently for Marleigh to return.

MARLEIGH PARKED HER car in front of the home where she'd purchased the portrait of Winston. It seemed so long ago now, though it had only been a month. She got out of the car, walked up to the door and knocked. Mentally, she kept rehearsing what she intended to say.

The door opened and Gertrude stood there holding an oven mitt. "May I help you?" she asked curiously.

"Hello," Marleigh said. "You may not remember me, but I purchased a portrait from you last month and my mother purchased a huge amount of depression glass."

"Of course," Gertrude said laughing. "Come in. Are you hoping for more depression glass? I can assure you that your mother bought all I had."

"I'm sure she did," Marleigh said as Gertrude gestured her to sit down. "I won't take up your time, ma'am. I was just wondering if you still had any of your father's possessions that you haven't yet sold."

Gertrude's eyes widened. "Well, I do have his books, but no other paintings I'm afraid. Why do you ask?"

"I was just hoping to add something vintage to my bedroom to go along with the portrait," Marleigh lied. "An old book would work."

"Of course," Gertrude said standing. "My father had a ton of books and they're in the garage after the last yard sale. I'll take you back there and you can look for yourself."

"I appreciate it," Marleigh replied following her to the back of the house. Her hopes rising higher than she thought they would.

Gertrude opened the side door. "They're right in here," she said stepping down.

Marleigh followed her and realized that they were in the attached garage just off from the kitchen. There were several boxes of books and other items littering the garage.

"Sorry about the mess," Gertrude said looking around. "Take your time. I'm right in the kitchen preparing dinner."

Marleigh nodded as she looked at the boxes and then began rummaging through them. Most of the books were old, but she didn't see anything that looked like a diary. She knew she had to choose something or Gertrude would be suspicious and she didn't want to be caught in a lie.

She spotted an old copy of Moby Dick and picked it up then set it aside as she combed through the last box of books. There was no diary. She picked up the copy of Moby Dick and headed back inside. Her hands were filthy and she needed to wash them. "I think I'll take this," she said as she walked back into the kitchen. Gertrude was standing over the stove and turned around.

"That's all you found," she asked wiping her hands.

"I need to wash my hands if you don't mind," Marleigh said holding them up. "Those books were quite dusty."

"Of course," Gertrude said pointing to the half bath just off from the kitchen. "Help yourself." She picked up the copy of Moby Dick. "Five dollars for the book."

Marleigh nodded then went into the bathroom and shut the door. *Now what?* The diary wasn't in the boxes and there was no way to ask Gertrude about it. She quickly washed her hands, grabbed a paper towel, and dried them as she opened the door.

Gertrude was humming as she stirred the pot she stood over.

Marleigh reached in her purse and pulled out a five-dollar bill.

"Here you go," she said placing the bill on the table. She picked up the book. "Thanks again."

"No problem," Gertrude said turning off the burner. "Are you enjoying Winston?"

Her question took Marleigh by surprise. "Winston?"

"You didn't know that soldier's name was Winston." Gertrude laughed. "Daddy talked to him all the time when I was growing up. He purchased it in England, you know. Daddy was a British soldier himself, and I guess it reminded him of home."

"Really," Marleigh said interested. "Yes, I'm enjoying Winston."

"Good, good," Gertrude said. "Daddy talked to him like he was a real person. In fact, he told me once that Winston was a real person. I just thought he was pulling my leg, but once when I was about fifteen, I heard two voices coming from the living room after I'd gone to bed. I asked Daddy about it the next day, and he said he was just talking to Winston. I guess he was using two voices." She laughed. "Daddy was a bit eccentric; you know."

Marleigh smiled. "Well, I don't use two voices when I talk to him, but I used to talk to myself before I bought him from you."

"Ah, well that explains it then," Gertrude replied picking up the money and placing it in her pocket.

Heading towards the front door, Marleigh tried to think of some way to ask her about the diary.

"Thanks for coming by," Gertrude said opening the door. "If you leave me your number, I'd be happy to let you know about the next sale. I still haven't cleaned out everything from Daddy's home and I'll be putting it on the market soon."

Marleigh perked up. "Really?" she asked, pulling out her note pad. "I'd like that. If you find any more books, or old ledgers, I'd appreciate it."

Gertrude nodded taking the paper from her. "Of course. In fact, I know that there are more books. Funny you should say ledger, because my daddy had a few as well as some old diaries that he once told me belonged to a witch." She laughed. "Daddy was always pulling my leg."

Marleigh tried to keep down the excitement she felt. "Really? I'd love to see any old witch ledgers. Promise me that I can get first dibs?"

"Of course," Gertrude said nodding. "I'll call you next week. If you'd like, you can meet me at Daddy's. That way, I don't have to haul all that stuff back here. My husband wanted me to just call the Salvation Army and let them pick up everything. Why would I do that when they are just going to turn around and sell it? I can sell it and make me some spare cash."

"Well, why not just sell it from there?" Marleigh asked.

"I cut the electric and water off after he died and the house is out in the sticks. I don't want to have to drive to a service station to pee."

Marleigh laughed. "I can understand that." She walked out the door and turned to Gertrude. "Thanks again and please call me when you're ready to go to your father's home."

"I will," Gertrude promised as she shut the door behind her.

Marleigh felt hopeful. There was a chance she would be able to get her hands on Temperance's diary, or is it diaries? Either way, she couldn't wait to tell Winston the good news.

Chapter Ten

MARLEIGH HEADED BACK to her car and was shocked to find Jett Graham leaning against it.

"Hello, there," he said grinning.

"What do you want, Mr. Graham" she snapped, barely civil.

"I happened to be in the neighborhood and saw your car," he said slyly. "I wrote down your plate number after your hasty departure from the park that day."

"I don't appreciate you stalking me," she said. "You're going to make me call the cops."

"I wasn't stalking you," he said coolly. "In fact, I was across the street doing an interview with Mr. Carl Clarkson when I noticed your car."

"Carl Clarkson, the gun nut that's been all over the news," Marleigh said disgusted. "Why am I not surprised."

"Well, you're entitled to your opinion and he's entitled to his second amendment rights." He gave her a smug look.

"Yes, it's just amazing to me that when blacks tried to carry guns to protect themselves back in the day as Black Panthers, they were described as a 'great threat to internal security to our country,' according to J. Edgar Hoover. Laws were then passed to restrict their rights to carry guns, but now every white gun nut can crawl from under a rock and spout off the second amendment."

"That was a different time," Jett responded, defensively.

"The only thing different is the color of their skin," Marleigh pointed out.

"The Black Panthers killed people," he pointed out.

Marleigh raised a brow and opened her car door. "You're forgetting about Charlottesville, aren't you?" She laughed when Jett didn't reply and got into her car.

"I still want to talk to Winston Spencer," Jett insisted. "When will I get my interview?"

"When hell freezes over," Marleigh said starting her engine. She looked in her rear-view mirror and watched him get small in her eyesight as she drove off.

WINSTON COULD SEE MARLEIGH was upset when she walked into the bedroom.

She threw down her purse and removed her jacket. She glanced at the television and then at him. "Winston, come forth," she said removing her shoes.

"You had company," he said as soon as he could.

"Company?" Marleigh asked surprised as she put on her slippers. "I noticed the TV was turned off."

"The man did it," Winston replied. "Two men came with a can, spraying something. They said they were fumigating?"

"Oh, I'd totally forgot about that," Marleigh replied. "The apartment sprays for bugs twice a year."

"I was wondering what they were about," Winston said removing his sword and hat. He sniffed the air. "I do not smell anything."

"It's odorless," Marleigh replied. "I picked up some Chinese food on the way home. I hope you like it."

"Chinese food?" Winston chuckled. "I have never eaten it. What does it consist of?"

"Mainly rice, some chicken and shrimp with vegetables." She removed the painting from the wall. "Come on, it's in the kitchen."

Winston followed her and sat at the table as she sat the portrait against the nearby oven.

Removing the white boxes from the brown bag on the table, she then placed a paper plate in front of him. She handed him a fork, took some rice from the box, and spooned it on his plate. Opening another box, she spooned out some shrimp mixed with vegetables and placed them on top of the white rice.

"It does smell good," he admitted. "I remember there were some China-men in my hometown. Most did laundry, but a few had small eating houses. We never ate there, of course."

Marleigh raised a brow. "Why not?"

"Well, because they were Chinese," Winston replied. "British people didn't eat Chinky food. They were looked down on as dirty foreigners."

"I see." Marleigh frowned.

"What is wrong, Marleigh?" he asked quietly.

"Look Winston, you may not realize this because you come from a different time. I know that I have to be patient with you, but you're prejudiced."

"Prejudiced?"

"You judge people by their race, Winston. You called them China-men and Chinks. No one says that! It's racist."

Winston dropped his fork, as her disapproval seemed to suck the oxygen out of the room. "I am truly sorry, Marleigh. Forgive me. What do you want me to do?" He was glad to see her face soften.

"I'm sorry too. I have to remember that you come from another time and things were different all those years ago. I guess I'm still upset because I ran into Jett Graham again."

"What!" Winston snapped. "Is he still following you?"

"He claimed that he was interviewing someone across the street from Gertrude's house when I went there—"

"Did you get the diary?" he asked interrupting her.

"No, but let me finish. I don't know whether I believe Jett Graham or not. He claimed he remembered my license plate number from that day in the park. I just know that I have to be careful, and I don't think we should go out. I don't trust that man."

"Of course," Winston agreed nodding.

"As for the diary, it wasn't at her home, but she did tell me that she still has more of her father's items at his home and she even said that she had some witch's ledgers."

"They must be Temperance's diaries!" Winston exclaimed.

"That's what I figured too," Marleigh agreed. "She's going to call me when she goes back to her father's home and I'll meet her there. Hopefully, I can get the diaries and I pray that she doesn't charge me that much."

Just then, a knock sounded on the front door.

"Now, who could that be?" Marleigh groaned. She stood up, looked through the peep hole and quickly pulled back. "It's him!"

"Who?"

"Jett Graham! He must have followed me here!" she seethed.

"Oh dear," Winston replied.

Before she could say more, he headed out of the kitchen and then disappeared. Marleigh sighed, knowing that he was safely back in the portrait. There was another hard knock and she quickly opened the door. "I'm calling the cops," she snapped at Jett Graham.

He didn't seem to care. "I'm not doing anything," he protested grinning. "You left rather abruptly, and I wanted to continue our conversation."

"We have nothing to talk about," Marleigh replied.

He looked over her shoulder. "Having dinner? Perhaps Winston Spencer is here."

"Do you see Winston Spencer?" she asked dryly. "I'm alone."

"There are two plates on your table," Jett pointed out.

"Yet, only one has food on it," Marleigh said icily. "The other plate just happens to be on the table. Two paper plates were stuck together. It happens all the time."

"Of course." Jett nodded. "Still, if you were having dinner with Mr. Spencer, we could get this over with and I'd be out of your hair."

"I told you that I don't want to give an interview," Marleigh said losing her patience. "Now would you please leave before I call the cops!" She tried to shut the door.

He grabbed it and flung it open, causing her to jump back. "You listen here, girl!" Jett growled. "I've been doing some checking on your friend. I couldn't find information on a Winston Spencer being legally admitted in this country! There's no record of him coming here legally. I can't find a visa or a green card. I know he must be an illegal alien and you're stupid to think that you can hide him for long."

"How dare you!" Marleigh cried. "Get out!"

"Why would you have a painting of a man you claim you hardly know?" Jett said walking over to Winston's portrait and picking it up. "In fact, he's wearing exactly the same thing he was wearing that day I saw you two in the park. You've been lying to me, Miss Winters. I know you're hiding something and I intend to find out what that is. I'm going to find him and then I'm going to have him deported if he can't present proper documentation."

"You get out of my house, right now!" Marleigh yelled looking around for her cell and realizing it was in the bedroom. She snatched Winston from his grasp. "Leave!"

"Fine, I'll go," Jett replied. "But be sure to read Friday's edition of the Post. You may find it very interesting." He walked out.

Marleigh slammed the door behind him. Her hands shook as she tried to calm herself. She put the chain on the door and peeked out the window just in time to see Jett Graham pulling off. "Winston, come forth."

"I say, he really is a cheeky tosser," Winston said shaking his head. "Maybe you should file a report for harassment."

"Maybe I will." Marleigh nodded.

Winston sat back down to eat. He looked up at her. "Sit down and eat, Marleigh," he said. "You can't worry about him."

"He said something was going to be in the paper Friday," she pointed out. "There's no telling what he'll print."

"Well, he cannot just print anything," Winston suggested reassuringly. "Aren't there laws against libel? What is he going to say? He cannot prove anything other than the fact that you have a painting of a man that he wants to interview, and that is not against the law."

"True," Marleigh said nodding.

"I heard him say that he can't find any paperwork on me, so what can he prove? He won't find any, at least not in this century."

Marleigh laughed. "I wouldn't put it past that fool to go looking into the history books."

"They will lock him up and throw away the key if he tries to convince people that a man from the 19th century is here illegally." He finished eating and pushed back his plate. "He has nothing to go on, Marleigh. You get those diaries and then we will be able to figure this out. And by the by, this Chinese food was utterly delicious," he said grinning at her.

Chapter Eleven

OVER THE NEXT FEW WEEKS, Marleigh was very careful. She didn't know if Jett was watching her or not, but she wasn't taking any chances.

She regretted not being able to take Winston outside, but she couldn't take that chance. She kept waiting patiently for Gertrude to call her so she could meet her and look for Temperance's diaries.

Of course, she'd been spending nights with Winston and she knew for sure that she was falling in love with him. How could she be falling in love with someone that wasn't even real? What would they do even if they were able to figure out the way to break the spell?

Winston wouldn't have any birth records or any way to even prove who he was and most likely, he would be deported. Deported to where though? There wouldn't be any records of him anywhere, at least no recent records.

She decided that perhaps she could go to the library and do some research into Winston's past, based on the information he'd given her. Maybe she could find out what happened to him after the portrait was painted. After all, he'd told her that Temperance had said that he'd lived a full life. Did he have children? Grandchildren? Great-grandchildren? The thought was mind boggling.

She'd taken a half day vacation from her job and was now sitting in the library, combing through records of Britain and her country's relationship during Winston's life time.

She knew he'd been born in 1874 and the portrait had been painted in 1895. He'd told her he'd wanted to be a correspondent while in Her Majesty's service, but he wasn't sure if he ever was.

Marleigh decided to do a search by his name and found nothing. What did she expect? There wasn't a lot of information on British soldiers unless they had some ties to America. Still, Winston had said his father's brother was the Duke of Newcastle. She then decided to search that name on the web to see what she could find.

She got a surprise when there was plenty of information on the Dukedom and she began to read all she'd found.

JETT GRAHAM GROANED as he glanced across the library at Marleigh. What was she doing and why was she here at the library?

Perhaps he was at a dead end with this girl, but for some reason, he couldn't let it go. He'd followed her around, hopefully without her finding out and had come up empty. She went to work, sometimes she visited her parents, but he hadn't spotted the elusive Winston Spencer. He'd watched her apartment, and there had been no sign of him.

The story he'd printed in the Post, which was a small local paper, hadn't generated that much attention. He'd only talked about the crisis of illegal aliens in the country and the many ways they were trying to take advantage of the gray areas of the law. He knew that The Post was a far-right publication that fed the fears and insecurities of Whites who wanted their country back. He snickered to himself. No, he didn't believe all their rantings, but it did sell advertising, and the digital subscriptions were doing well.

He moved closer to the table where Marleigh was working, careful to stay out of view. He watched as she pulled up an old black and white video and barely heard her low gasp as she leaned in for a closer look at the grainy image on the screen.

He could tell that she was a bit rattled and watched as she quickly logged out of whatever she'd been watching and nervously gathered up her things. What in the world could have gotten her so upset?

For a moment, he was unsure whether to follow her as she left, or remain and try to find out what she had been watching. Hell, he'd been following her for weeks! He walked over to the table where she'd sat. Maybe she'd left some sort of clue he could use.

The table was clear, but he did notice the nearby wastebasket and walked over to it. Several pieces of notepad paper had been wadded up and discarded which he quickly confiscated. He sat down, opened them and spread them on the table.

There wasn't much on either paper. WW1 was scratched through and then the word correspondent. Nothing else was on that paper. He looked at the second piece of paper which said Duke of Newcastle and then the words seventh Duke. What could that mean? Nothing else was written on the paper and he turned it over only to find that the back was blank. He couldn't be sure the writing even belonged to Miss Winters. Maybe these discarded notes weren't even hers.

Still, something had upset the girl. Who was this Duke of Newcastle? Could it have something to do with Winston Spencer? He quickly opened his laptop and did his own search.

The Duke of Newcastle was a dukedom that went back to the time of Queen Anne and had been bestowed upon a man named Sir Alexander Spencer in the year 1706. He'd been a soldier and later, the country's Prime Minister.

Jett stared at the painting of the duke who wore a long white wig. Perhaps this man was a descendant of Winston Spencer. He looked through the list that named the Dukes of Newcastle, but could find no Winston Spencer among them.

He continued to comb through articles pertaining to the Dukedom, but found nothing of interest. His gut kept telling him something was here, but what?

He glanced at a link to the Dukedom's family tree and pulled it up. It showed a portrait of the first Duke and those after him. He then looked back at the scribbling on the paper that said seventh duke. Could this be a clue? He scrolled down to the seventh Duke of Newcastle whose name was John Spencer and noted that he had nine children! He combed through the names of the nine, but none of them was named Winston Spencer.

He was about to give up, when he noticed a search box on the tree. He quickly entered the name Winston Spencer and was taken to a page which had a more detailed tree with John Spencer at the top, leading down to Winston Spencer which was his great grandson born in 1874. Obviously, this Winston Spencer must be a descendant of the one he was now hunting, and he quickly clicked on the link embedded in the name.

He was shocked when he was taken to the exact portrait he'd held in his hands of the young man in uniform a few weeks earlier at her apartment. He enlarged it on the computer screen, staring at it in shock. What did this mean? Why did Miss Winters have a copy of this portrait in her possession? The Winston Spencer he'd met had to be a relative of this man! He looked at the descendants of Winston Spencer and found that there was a present-day Winston Spencer, but he was over fifty years old and he had no sons.

Jett closed the laptop and his head began to throb. Obviously, the man in the park had been an imposter, but to what end? Why did he have the portrait of the real Winston Spencer in his possession? He didn't know, but he was certainly going to make it his business to find out.

MARLEIGH HURRIED INTO her apartment and locked the door. She threw her purse on a nearby chair and headed to the bedroom. She sat on the bed and called Winston forth as she began to take off her shoes.

"I say, you are home early," Winston said grinning at her. He set his hat down which he called his bearskin as well as his sword, and walked over to her.

"I went to the library and did some research on your family," she admitted. She watched as his eyes widened and quickly continued, "I figured that there may be some information that we could use if the spell is able to be broken."

Winston grew solemn and stood in front of her with his hands behind his back. "Go on."

"Well, it seems you were an important man in your later years," Marleigh began. "You were a war correspondent in the Daily Star newspaper as well a correspondent for the BBC on television."

"You don't say," Winston replied, clearly surprised.

"Yes, and you received numerous awards for your journalism," Marleigh continued. "I was able to pull up an old video online and I saw you. You were older, but your voice was the same. You tend to drag out your 's' when you speak. Would you like to see it?"

Winston stepped back and looked out the window with his back to her. "No, not now...maybe later. Did I marry?"

Marleigh knew that he would ask, and she cleared her throat. "Yes, you had one son and three daughters. Of course, they've all passed, but from what I can gather from the information I found, you still have family in Great Britain."

Winston turned to her. "I can never go back there. I do not want to hear any more about that. Was I happy? Did I have a good life?"

Marleigh nodded, "Yes, from what I could find, you did."

"Good," Winston said sitting on the bed beside her. He took her hand in his. "Marleigh, that was another life, and while I am glad that it was a good one and that apparently I was a good man, a good husband and father... I don't remember any of it. Even if this spell can be broken, where does that leave me? I cannot go home, and I certainly cannot find my family. But what would I tell them? No, my life now is here with you."

Marleigh pulled her hand from his. "We don't even know if there will be a life together for us, Winston."

"We will have to find those diaries to know that," Winston agreed. He took her hand back in his. "Do you feel that you cannot be with me because I was married to someone else?" he asked.

"No, that's not it," Marleigh said shaking her head. "I mean, you're right. You can't go back and be the Winston Spencer you were before. That person is dead and gone. You will have to make a new life for yourself, if that's at all possible."

Winston stood up. "First things first. We have to get those diaries."

WINSTON HELD MARLEIGH in his arms as she slept. He was surprised she was sleeping so peacefully. She had been upset by the information she'd found online about him. He did not totally understand modern day computers, but he was learning.

The large amount of information now stored on computers amazed him. The amount that just a chip held would have taken up space in buildings as large as the House of Lords and the House of Commons combined. It was mind boggling how information could be found at a click of a button.

He had felt glad that his former self had lived a good life, but he wanted his present and future life to be lived with Marleigh, he just was not sure how it could be done. He pulled her closer and inhaled her scent. She was his everything now, and he did not want imagine a life without her.

He could not lose her, nor did he want to be trapped in that painting and watch her grow older while he remained the same as he was now. The answers had to be in those diaries!

He could not see her clearly, but he felt her move in his arms and her fingers caress his face.

"You're restless," she whispered.

"I am fine," he countered.

She picked up her phone from the nightstand and the light from it invaded the room as she touched the screen.

He could see on the phone screen that it was a little after 2 am.

"I was thinking," she said as she put the phone back on the night-stand. "Maybe I should call Gertrude. It has been a few weeks after all."

"You do not think she will mind? Maybe she has been busy."

"Well it won't hurt to ask," Marleigh insisted.

"I was hoping you would say that," he admitted. "I feel those diaries are the key to our future."

"Of course, I have to keep an eye out for Jett Graham." She sighed. "I've been reading that racist tabloid of his, The Post. Thankfully, our names weren't mentioned in that last article of his, but I know he's still looking for a breakthrough for his story about illegal aliens."

Winston kissed her forehead. "He has not mentioned us, because he does not have anything worth printing, and he knows it. He can't find anything on me because I do not exist, at least not in this day and time."

"Still, I don't trust him," Marleigh insisted. "I feel like it's only a matter of time before that fool stumbles onto something, and then what?"

Winston shook his head. "We shall deal with that fool when the time comes. In the meantime, let's concentrate on those diaries."

TWO DAYS PASSED, AND Marleigh was excited when her phone vibrated while she was working and she saw it was Gertrude. Unfortunately, she was in the middle of teaching her class and couldn't answer it.

She thought she would go crazy wondering what Gertrude had said. Finally, she grabbed her phone when she put the kids down for their afternoon nap. Almost holding her breath, she listened to the message.

Gertrude informed her that she would be out at her father's house this weekend and that Marleigh could meet her there on Saturday if she wished.

Marleigh quickly texted her telling her she would meet her at whatever time she wanted, and for Gertrude to please send her the address, so she could put it in her GPS.

Gertrude texted her back to immediately confirm their meeting. At last, they were making some progress!

Saturday was two days away, and she hoped Gertrude would find the diaries, so she and Winston could find a way to break the spell.

Chapter Twelve

MIDDLEBURG, VA WAS less than fifty miles from Washington, DC. Marleigh was surprised by the large estates she passed as she followed the GPS to the address Gertrude had given her.

She pulled into the driveway of a yellow two-story home with a bay window and knew she had arrived because she recognized Gertrude's car. So, this was the place where Winston had lived with Miles. She got out of the car and set the alarm.

Gertrude opened the front door. "You made it!" she exclaimed. "Did you have any problems finding me?"

"No," Marleigh said walking into the modest home. "I passed all these huge estates and I wondered if one of them was yours."

"Not a chance." Gertrude laughed. "My father wasn't rich, and he built this home himself. It's prime property and I have numerous inquiries, though I haven't even put it on the market yet. One man offered me $800,000 right off the bat. I mean really? This place only has three bedrooms and two and a half baths! I can only imagine what those big barns you passed are selling for."

Marleigh looked around the spacious home. "It's beautiful," she admitted, admiring the marble top tables she saw. "Did you grow up here?"

"Yes." Gertrude sighed. "I loved it here. I don't want to sell it, though my husband has been pressuring me because of the amount of taxes I have to pay on this place. So, we compromised. I'm gonna rent it to cover the taxes and make a little money, after I remove all Papa's things. I've sold some and put the items I'm giving to my children in storage. Now, come on upstairs and I'll show you the books that are still here."

Marleigh followed her up the steps to the bedroom at the top of the stairs. She spotted the boxes of books immediately at the foot of the bed.

"Help yourself," Gertrude said smiling. "Take your time. I'll be downstairs if you have any questions."

Marleigh swiftly went through the boxes and found several old binders made of pale worn and faded vellum, bound with cloth ties. The binders were stab sewn through the vellum to bind the book, along with a flap and two cloth ties used to tie the binder closed. Her hands shook a little as she opened it.

The writing looked to be neatly handwritten with exquisite penmanship that rivaled any calligraphy she'd ever seen. The penmanship was bold and neat, yet faded. She quickly set it aside and found three more, noting that the handwriting in each was the same. Her heart beat hard in her chest. She had to get these to Winston so the two of them could go through them together.

She hurried down the steps and called out to Gertrude.

"In here," Gertrude responded.

Marleigh followed her voice and found her in a sun room in the back of the house.

Gertrude had made a pot of tea there were two porcelain cups on the table with it. "Sit, sit," she insisted as she poured herself a cup. She looked at the binders Marleigh was holding. "I see you found something. I remember those; a bunch of gibberish." Gertrude rolled her eyes. "Didn't make a damn bit of sense to me."

"How much?" Marleigh said sipping her tea.

"One hundred bucks each. They're quite old," Gertrude responded, looking over her cup.

Marleigh began to cough. "One hundred dollars! I don't have that kind of money!"

"Such a pity," Gertrude said sitting down her cup. "I have another gentleman who wants to look at them, but I'd promised them to you first. He's already offered me that much."

"How could he? When he hasn't seen them," Marleigh insisted.

"Oh, he claims to be some sort of expert on witches. I snapped a few pictures of the cover of each book as well as the first five pages from them, and sent them to him in a text and he immediately made the offer."

Marleigh looked down at the books. She wanted to cry. She had to have them to save Winston! Who was this expert? "How did he find out about the books," Marleigh asked suspiciously.

Gertrude poured herself another cup of tea. "Well, after my last yard sale, you know the one where your mother bought all that depression glass, my son suggested that I put some of my Daddy's stuff on eBay and it would sell just as well, without me having to haul it outside. I thought it was a great idea, so I did it for about twenty of the books remaining in Daddy's room as well as some other items. I just snapped a few pictures of the covers with the titles, and lo and behold, I got the request asking me to send a few pictures of the first few pages of each one. Then, bam! He made me an offer."

Marleigh held the books possessively. She wasn't about to let anyone else get these books. They were hers.... hers and Winston's. She had to figure out something. "I do want them," Marleigh replied. "I had no idea that you had another offer. When we talked, you never mentioned it."

"That's true," Gertrude said nodding. "I had already talked to you when my son made the suggestion to try eBay. Of course, I couldn't sell them until I gave you a chance to buy them, because Daddy always said, 'Your word is your bond,' so I had to offer you the books first."

"I don't have four hundred dollars," Marleigh confessed, "but I do want them, please Gertrude, can we work something out?"

Gertrude sighed. "Look Marleigh, this is business. The man has already offered me four hundred, and I can't sell them to you for less."

"Please," Marleigh begged. "There must be something I can do?"

Gertrude rubbed her eyes and Marleigh could see that she was thinking.

"I tell you what," she said finally. "Four hundred dollars is my price, but I could use some help around here moving and shipping some of Daddy's things that I sell on eBay. My son said he'd help me, but he has his own family to deal with. However, I've put the utilities back on, so I can work from here instead of my home. If you can help me with that on a consistent basis, then we have a deal."

Marleigh jumped up and hugged her. "Oh, thank you, Gertrude!"

Gertrude pulled away from her. "Now before you get all thankful, I want you to give me your personal information, a copy of your driver's license and I'll write up a contract. I don't want you skipping out on me. I want a copy of your car's registration too and your job information."

"No problem," Marleigh said grinning.

"Also, you can't have the books until you've paid off your debt."

Marleigh's shoulders dropped. She wanted to take those books home today! She looked at Gertrude and knew she wouldn't be changing her mind. Why should she when she had a buyer ready to pay cash? "I can pay for one now," she said slowly.

"Good," Gertrude said smiling. "Pick one and give me the other three. I'll lock them up safe like and I won't sell them to anyone else. You can work off the remaining $300 if you can't come up with it. I'll give you $20 an hour towards your debt. I think that's fair, don't you?"

"Yes, very fair." Marleigh opened each of the books and realized the pages were dated. After glancing at the first pages of each of the books, she put them in date order. She noticed that inside the cover of each was written, 'Diary of Temperance Rice'. She then took the oldest and reluctantly handed Gertrude the others.

"Now mind you, I'm a workaholic myself, and I expect you to work for that $20. Don't try to shortchange me," she said taking the books from Marleigh.

"I won't," Marleigh said shaking Gertrude's extended hand. She stood on her feet. "I work during the week and I can help you on weekends."

"Well, you already here now," Gertrude pointed out. "It's early, not even noon yet. How much time can you give me today?"

Marleigh peered down at her phone. If she could work five hours, she could take two books home instead of just one. "I can start now and I'll work five hours to pay for another book," she offered.

Gertrude smiled. "I was hoping you'd say that."

Marleigh wished she could somehow get in touch with Winston and tell him the news, but knew he was in the painting and there was no way to contact him. She sighed and locked the book in her trunk after sending Gertrude the payment electronically. She would get through the day and hoped some of the answers they were seeking were in the first two books.

She walked back into the house and immediately saw Gertrude who was staring at her phone concerned.

"Is everything all right?" she asked.

"Yes," Gertrude said looking up at her. "I texted the other buyer, giving him my apologies, and telling him that the books had been sold to my first client. He then turned around and offered me a thousand dollars for all four books if I would break our contract and sell them to him instead."

"What!" Marleigh gasped. "You're going to sell them to him?"

"Of course not, we have a deal," Gertrude replied smugly. "Besides, something's off with this guy. He asked for more pictures of the pages and even offered me the thousand dollars if I copy all the pages and send them to him."

"What are you going to do?" Marleigh asked. "You could copy all the pages, sell the books to me, and still make another thousand dollars. Is that what you're going to do?"

"No," Gertrude said shaking her head. "I've already made my deal and if he wants copies, he'll have to get them from you. I didn't share your name with him though. I haven't answered him yet. I wanted to talk to you first."

"Of course," Marleigh said breathing a sigh of relief.

"Besides," Gertrude said leading her back upstairs, "I found a gambling note in my father's things while you were working. It seems that he won those books and the portrait of Winston together back in England from a man named Thomas Rice. The note did have a stipulation that Thomas Rice could pay his debt of five hundred pounds and get his property back within ninety days, but Daddy had left England by then. That tells me that the books go with the painting and I knew that you should have them."

"Five hundred pounds?" Marleigh asked. "What was the date on the receipt?"

I think it was March of 1936," Gertrude said. "I was just four years old at the time. I'm surprised that my father took the portrait and binders, instead of that money which was over six hundred dollars in US currency, but then again, Daddy could be a little eccentric." She shook her head.

"Maybe it was because he had to leave England and come here," Marleigh pointed out. "Maybe he'd already purchased his plane ticket."

"We came by ship," Gertrude said. "I remember it a little because Mama was sea sick, but not me and Daddy. He told me that I was a real sailor. Now..." She placed her hands on her hips. "Enough chatter. Let's get to work."

MARLEIGH GROANED. SHE ached all over. Gertrude hadn't been kidding when she'd said that she was a workaholic. That old woman ran circles around her. Marleigh had never seen a woman that age with so much energy.

She didn't regret it though. The hard work had earned her the second book. She watched as the FedEx truck pulled up to pick up the packages that she'd prepared. There were several lamps that she'd carefully wrapped, some other books, two rugs, a cedar chest and some old British coins. That cedar chest had been tricky. It wasn't that heavy, but it was bulky and they had struggled to get it into the crate for shipping.

Gertrude handed her the second book. "Here, you earned it."

"Thanks," Marleigh said taking it from her. She then walked out to her car and opened the trunk, placing the book in the cloth bag with the other.

The FedEx man was checking in the packages and turned to her. "I know that you didn't lift that box and bring it out here by yourself," the man said shaking his head.

"It's not that heavy," Marleigh reassured him. "It's just big. See for yourself."

The FedEx driver took the dolly, loaded the box, and wheeled it back to the truck. He then gave her a grin.

Marleigh walked back into the house and found Gertrude in the kitchen. "Well, I'm about to leave," she said. "It'll be dark in an hour and I want to get home."

"Of course," Gertrude said smiling. "I'm about to leave myself. Let me lock up."

Marleigh nodded and was heading to the door when there was a knock. Thinking it was the FedEx man, she opened the door.

Instead, a tall, stocky man with thick eyebrows stared at her. His hair was a mass of unruly salt and pepper curls and his eyes were a pale gray.

"May I help you?" she asked, looking over his shoulder and realizing that the FedEx man had left.

"Yes, I'm here to see Gertrude Wright," the man insisted, almost snarling.

Marleigh knew at once he was British, and that he didn't look too friendly. "Wait here," she said quickly shutting the door.

"Who was that?" Gertrude asked as she put her purse on her shoulder.

"It's some British guy looking for you," Marleigh said. "Is he the buyer?"

"I don't know. I didn't give him this address," Gertrude replied.

Marleigh stepped back as she opened the door.

"May I help you," Gertrude asked looking up at the man.

"Gertrude Wright?"

"That's right, how may I help you?"

"I'm Tim Hale, I spoke to you...well, I talked to you by text message about the books."

Gertrude nodded. "I see. Mr. Hale, I told you in my last message that I'd sold the books to the first buyer who made me an offer. I don't know how you found my address, but I'm sorry you came all this way for nothing."

He looked at Marleigh. "Is this the one?"

"The one?" Gertrude asked playing dumb.

"The one who bought my books?" he snapped.

"Oh, no," Gertrude responded before Marleigh could reply. "This girl is my help. Now if you would, Mr. Hale, I need you to leave. The books have been purchased and the buyer has gone on his way."

"Who is he?" Tim demanded.

"Sir, if you don't leave as my employer has asked you, I'm calling the cops," Marleigh said, pulling out her phone.

"Hey, don't get your knickers in a bunch," Tim insisted. "I'm just asking. I told you that I'd pay you a thousand dollars for photocopies of the pages of those books. That should be easy money."

"I know you did," Gertrude said giving him her best smile. "In fact, I've called the buyer after you made your offer and I'm just waiting for him to call me back."

Tim Hale's, face seemed to soften. He handed her a card. "Here's my cellular number. Call me when you get what I want," he said looking from Gertrude to Marleigh.

"Of course," Gertrude responded.

Chapter Thirteen

WINSTON WONDERED WHAT was keeping Marleigh so long. Had she gotten lost trying to find Gertrude's house?

The sun had set and he'd watched all the news he could stand. He remained stuck in this blasted painting and Marleigh could be out there hurt somewhere. He tried to concentrate on what was being said on the telly, but he couldn't help thinking about her, and worrying. The room was growing dimmer by the minute and soon, the only light would be from the telly. It was late in the evening. She'd been gone since morning.

He felt a weight lift off his chest as he heard the key in the lock.

Marleigh flicked on the light in the bedroom and tossed a cloth bag on the bed. She walked over to the telly, picked up the remote and cut it off.

She called him from the painting and he quickly set down his hat and sword. He grabbed her in a tight hug. "I was so worried," he said releasing her.

"I know, I couldn't help it," Marleigh said. She quickly told him about her day and about her contract with Gertrude. "Then a man came by demanding the books!" Marleigh said finishing her story. "Gertrude told him that the buyer had already purchased them and I thought the man was going to lose it right there. But she promised him that she'd get him copies."

"What!" Winston responded surprised. "Why would she do that?"

"To get rid of him, I guess," Marleigh shrugged. "He was a scary looking character."

"That is not good for Gertrude. He may come back," Winston pointed out.

"I know. I think she just said that to get rid of him. He offered her a thousand dollars for copies. Isn't that crazy? Gertrude said that I could make the copies if I wanted and get the money."

"I do not think it is a good idea." Winston replied.

Marleigh pulled the two books out of the bag. "Me either," she agreed. "I only have the first two, but I was hoping that they may tell us something."

Winston sat on the bed beside her as she opened the first binder.

March 14, 1874

Rennie's gone and got off with some dollymop and now John Thomas and knackers are in trouble. It's bad enough that rich girl got knapped before, now he wants my help. He was half rats when I saw him. "Don't sell me a dog," I says. He begs, the nob does. I don't budge.

Marleigh looked at Winston. "I don't have any idea what I just read. Now I understand what Gertrude meant. This doesn't make a bit of sense and it says nothing about the spell that was cast."

Winston took the book from her. "I understand it."

"You do?" Marleigh asked surprised.

"It is British slang, from my time. Let me translate." He reread the entry and looked at her. "Someone named Rennie had sex with a loose woman and now, he apparently has caught a disease. Temperance has no sympathy for him because he got some rich girl pregnant, apparently before the incident with the loose woman. He then came to her half drunk, telling her lies, but she wouldn't help him. Apparently, Rennie is a titled gentleman."

"No wonder Gertrude said it was gibberish," Marleigh said shaking her head. "I'll let you read it and then you can tell me what it means." She lay back on the bed.

Winston rapidly combed through the pages. After ten minutes, he closed the first book. "Nothing about spells is in there. Mostly it is about Rennie coming to her with his disease. Then she talks about him marrying the rich girl, but still he was sleeping with prostitutes."

"Even with the disease?" Marleigh gasped.

"Apparently so," Winston replied.

"I feel for his poor wife," Marleigh grumbled. "He probably gave her the disease."

"No, he did not," Winston said rubbing his eyes and tossing the book on the bed. "As soon as I started reading, I realized who she was talking about. My mother didn't catch it and I learned that they stopped having relations after she became pregnant with my brother who is only ten months younger than myself."

"Are you sure?"

"Yes, I am sure that Rennie is my father. His name is Randolph," Winston said distastefully. "My mother is the rich girl and my father died of syphilis. It was not hard for me to put that together since Temperance bought the portrait from my mother's estate."

"Maybe we should call it a night," Marleigh said taking the book from his hands and slipping it back in the cloth bag.

"Yes, I believe you are right," Winston said smiling at her. He knew she was worried about how all this was affecting him.

"I've had a long day," she said standing. "I want a nice hot shower and then bed. I'm sore from all the work Gertrude got out of me today."

Winston smiled. "When you come out, I will rub you down with some liniment if you would like," he offered.

"I'd like that," she sighed, walking into the bathroom.

WINSTON LAY IN BED listening to Marleigh's breathing as she slept. He thought about all he had read in the first book.

Apparently, his father and Temperance were close, but not lovers. She hadn't written what the nature of their relationship was, but he could tell the two of them were close.

None of it made any sense, and he hoped the second book would shed some light on their relationship.

He'd done the math long ago and realized his mother must have been pregnant when she married his father. She was rich and he was a second son of a Duke, so apparently their indiscretion was overlooked. They'd grown up privileged with the help of the money from his mother's family. Had his father angered Temperance and then she'd cast the spell as some sort of revenge?

He wanted to look at the second book and see what it revealed.

"What's wrong?" Marleigh asked sleepily. "You're tense."

"I am sorry," he said kissing her. "I was just thinking..."

"I can imagine," she said sitting up and turning on the light. "Why don't I move you to the kitchen so you can read the second book?" She glanced at her phone. "I have to get up in a couple of hours anyway."

"I would like that," Winston replied honestly. "I can't stop thinking about it and wondering what is in the second book."

Marleigh rose and picked up the portrait.

Winston grabbed the book from the cloth bag and followed her to the kitchen.

She propped the portrait against the stove. "Make yourself comfortable. I'm going back to bed and you can fill me in when I get up."

"Of course," Winston agreed. He watched her as she walked out of the room and then opened the second book.

June 1, 1886

Rennie came to see me. He was poked up bringing me a bag of mystery. I took it. I ain't no church bell, and he knows it. He just sat and stared at his hands. He told me he copped a mouse after telling his wife. I didn't think the girl had it in her. I asked if he was still out on the pull and I thought he'd smack me. I can't help him. I'm still learning my way and told him so. I may have been born on the other side of the blanket, but I do care for Rennie.

Winston realized from the entry that Temperance must be a blood relative of some sort. His father had visited her and told her that his mother had given him a black eye when he told her about being infected. Well, good for her. Temperance said she was still learning and couldn't help him, asking his father if he was still cheating. Did she mean she was in witch training, if there was such a thing?

He continued to read the entries and realized that Temperance was in fact, learning to be a witch. She wrote that she was looking for a spell that could be a remedy for his father's syphilis, but hadn't been able to find one.

The last few entries talked about his father's death and how it had affected her. Winston could tell that Temperance was grieving. She wrote that she intended find a way to bring his father back. If that were the case, then why did she cast the spell on his portrait, and not the one of his father? Nothing was making much sense, and he needed the other two books to try to figure things out.

MARLEIGH HURRIED TO her car. She was about to get another written warning if she ended up late for work. She already had two and the third would turn into a suspension at this point. Her perfect record had gone down the toilet since Winston had come into her life, but she didn't give a rat's ass. She drove to work, praying that the traffic would be agreeable.

Winston had filled her in on the writings in the second binder, telling her that apparently Temperance had been family and had tried to find a cure for his father's syphilis. She couldn't muster up any sympathy for a man who was sleeping around while knowing he had a disease with no cure at the time.

She looked at her watch and realized she would make it to work on time. She quickly parked and exited her car, only to turn around and almost bump into someone.

Jett Graham had been standing behind her.

"What the hell?" she exclaimed, surprised.

"Miss Winters, we need to talk," he said calmly, eying her.

"Look, I'm due to punch in in three minutes," Marleigh said looking at her phone. "It will have to wait."

"Fine," Jett said as he followed her. "I'll meet you on your lunch break. What time is that?"

"I only get thirty minutes," Marleigh said reaching the door of the day care at the Children's Museum. "I don't want to talk about my personal business here."

"Well, I'll meet you when you get off," Jett insisted.

Marleigh glanced down at her phone. She had three minutes to punch in and didn't have time to argue with this fool. "Fine," she said opening the door. "Meet me here at five."

JETT GRAHAM SMIRKED as he watched Marleigh hurry inside the building. He knew she would agree since it appeared she was about to be late for work.

He'd been watching her, and knew she reported to work at 9 AM. He could tell she had been running late as he watched her apartment. Things had worked out just as he'd planned.

He'd done more research on the Spencer family and couldn't find any record of any of them being in the country, yet this Winston Spencer was the spitting image of the portrait. Could he be mistaken? He thought the man had looked exactly like the Winston Spencer in the portrait, but now he wasn't so sure. He needed to see him again face to face, but Marleigh Winters was hiding something. Maybe she didn't know where he was or what he was doing in the country, but why did she have the portrait? This was the key to this mystery, and he was determined to get some answers.

He doubled back to Marleigh's apartment hoping there was some way he could gain access in order to look around. He'd noticed a maintenance man the other day and perhaps he could bribe him.

He got out of his vehicle and noticed a large man standing at her door and knocking. He walked up to the man wondering who he was. "She's not home. She's at work," he said casually.

The man turned around giving Jett a curious stare. "Who are you," he snapped.

Jett noticed he had papers in his hands, which were large and meaty.

The cotton shirt he wore looked tight and the buttons strained as if they were about to pop any second. He was clean shaven, but had curly locks and needed a haircut. The man pushed his salt and pepper hair back from his face impatiently. "I said, who are you?" he snarled.

"I'm a friend of hers," Jett replied. "Who are you?"

"Are you the bloke who bought the books?" the man asked.

Jett didn't know what the man was talking about, but decided to play along. "No, I'm not" he responded. "But I probably can find out who did."

"Is that so?" the man asked eying him. "I offered her boss, Gertrude Wright a thousand dollars for copies of those books. I followed your girl from Middleburg on Saturday. I could tell that she knew something, but didn't want to say anything in front of her boss. Here's my card," he said handing it to Jett. "You tell her that Tim Hale came by and that I'll pay her the money if she gets me those copies."

"Does this have anything to do with the portrait of the soldier?" Jett asked.

"Portrait?" Tim asked narrowing his eyes. "She has the portrait of Winston Spencer?"

Jett immediately regretted giving out this information. "No, she said something about someone purchasing it from her employer. Maybe it was the same man who bought the books you're looking for."

Tim nodded in agreement. "I know about that portrait. You tell her that I'll pay her a finder's fee if she can direct me to the one who bought it. I doubt that it was the same one who bought the books. It's my understanding from Gertrude Winter's husband that the portrait was bought by someone at a yard sale, almost two months ago."

Jett stared at the man opened mouthed, but quickly caught himself. He looked at the card the man had handed him. "So...you're here dealing in antiquities?" he asked. "Are you from England?"

"Yes, I'm from Oxfordshire," Tim replied pushing past Jett. "You tell that girl what I said. You tell her to call me, or I'll be back over here!"

"What do these books you want have to do with the portrait?" Jett asked, trying to piece the puzzle together.

"Don't you worry about that," Tim snapped. "You just give that girl the message."

Jett watched him walk back to his car and then hurried to his own. He couldn't wait until he talked to Miss Marleigh Winters later that day.

Chapter Fourteen

MARLEIGH DREADED MEETING Jett, but knew she would have to in order to get rid of him.

When she came out of the building, she found him standing by her car grinning like that cat about to pounce on a helpless mouse. He wore that stupid worn cap, but today he had on a suit that didn't fit him properly.

She drew herself up and walked over to him, fueled by the anger she tried to contain. "So, what's this all about?" she asked.

"Let's go have dinner. I'm paying," Jett replied. "I've even dressed for the part."

"I don't want to have dinner with you," Marleigh snapped. "Just speak your mind."

"Are you sure you want to do this here?" Jett asked, looking around. "We are in the parking lot of your employer."

"Fine," she conceded. "Meet me at the convenience store across the street. I have to get some gas anyway."

Jett looked across the street where she pointed. "You sure you wouldn't rather get a free meal? If not, we could always go to your apartment for complete privacy." He gave her a hopeful stare.

"I don't think so," Marleigh said, glaring at him. "I don't trust you, so let's get this over with." She hurriedly got in the car and took off without looking back. Pulling into traffic, she quickly made a left at the light and drove into the convenience store with Jett Graham following her. She pulled in a parking space farthest from the door of the store and got out.

People were coming and going as no one paid her the slightest bit of attention. She was glad the parking lot was larger than that of most convenience stores. "So, what is this all about," she asked as she watched him exit his vehicle.

"It's about Winston Spencer," Jett began while pulling out his notepad.

"I told you that I don't know where he lives and that I don't know his number either," Marleigh insisted. "Why are you still beating this dead horse?"

"Maybe because you have a portrait of the real Winston Spencer in your possession." He eyed her triumphantly, pushing the cap on his head back a bit.

Marleigh tried to hide her surprise. "So, what if I do? I purchased that portrait."

"I know, at a yard sale," Jett continued as he smiled at her slyly. "There was a man who came to your apartment looking for some books and asking about the portrait."

"What man?"

"A big burly Brit," Jett replied. He looked away and chuckled to himself. "Big, burly, Brit. That's a tongue teaser."

"What did he want?" Marleigh asked impatiently.

"He said that he followed you from your employer's place in Middleburg, Virginia." He grinned at her. "I didn't know you were working another job. What were you doing in Middleburg?"

"My personal business is none of your concern," Marleigh said icily. "What were you doing at my apartment?"

"Well, I just happened to drive by there when I left you this morning. I saw him at your door and just had to investigate."

"You had to actually drive into my complex and be in the parking lot in order to see him at my door," Marleigh pointed out.

"True," Jett replied without a hint of embarrassment. "I was being nosy, but you can thank me now if you'd like."

"Look," she said patiently. "This is getting out of hand. Stop following me and stop coming to my apartment! I've given you sufficient warnings, so now I'm going to report you for stalking."

"You have more to worry about from that Brit than you do me," Jett said laughing. "He's ready to pay you for the painting and for locating some books he's looking for. He seemed quite fierce and a bit angry. You are going to have to watch out for that one for sure." He studied her a moment when she didn't respond. "You do know what books he's talking about; I presume," he pressed on. "He believes that you know what he's talking about."

"So, what if I do?" Marleigh replied. "What's in this for you?"

"A story, of course. Now tell me, how is your friend, Winston Spencer connected to all this?" He held up his hand before she could answer. "Let me point out that the big burly Brit, who by the way, says his name is Tim Hale is going to come back. He said he followed you home on Saturday and he seemed pretty anxious about those books, so if you're going to report anyone for stalking, it should be him. At least, you know I'm harmless...not too sure about him though."

Marleigh could no longer hide her worried expression. Jett was watching her closely, but she struggled to remain calm. "Look, I can handle my own business," she insisted. "Give it a rest."

"I doubt if he's going to give up easily," Jett continued, eying her. "I can help you, if you would only help me."

"What do you want?" Marleigh sighed.

"What I've always wanted, a story," Jett insisted. "I have enough information to make up something on my own, but I want to hear it from the man himself. Can you get in touch with your Winston Spencer and have him meet me?"

"If I find him," Marleigh replied, "And that's a big if, what's in it for me?"

"I have resources to check out this Tim Hale and see if he's on the up and up. I have a friend in ICE who owes me a favor. In the meantime, I can distract Tim Hale and send him on a wild goose chase. Do you know where these books are that he's looking for?"

"I know who has them," Marleigh said evasively.

"He thinks you're working for some woman, Gertrude Wright in Middleburg, Virginia. Why is that?"

Marleigh stared at him as he consulted his notes and then looked at her expecting an answer. She decided to indulge him a bit. "She's a friend and I was helping her pack up some things. She's an older woman and needed some help."

"Ah, well I guess you were there then when Mrs. Wright sold the books he's looking for."

"Yes, but she sent them by FedEx to the buyers while I was there," Marleigh lied.

"Who was the buyer?" Jett asked.

"I don't remember exactly. There were three different ones," Marleigh said nervously as he kept watching her closely. She wasn't a very good liar and knew Jett would be able to see right through her. "I prepared the packages for shipping while I was there. Mrs. Wright had me box them up and print off the FedEx labels for pick up. I don't remember the addresses exactly. I believe they were being sent to Alexandria, Richmond and a place in North Carolina."

She eyed Jett who was writing everything down. What she told him wasn't a lie; she had mailed books off to those locations, just not the books Tim Hale was looking for.

"Very well," Jett responded. "I'll get him off your back and I'll get those addresses from Mrs. Wright. I'll pass the information along to him. In the meantime, I expect you to set up the interview I want."

"How will you do that?" Marleigh asked in disbelief. "I doubt if Gertrude will just up and give them to you."

"Don't you worry about that," Jett said smugly. "Just get me my interview."

WINSTON LISTENED WITHOUT interruption as Marleigh told him what had happened. He had heard someone talking outside after she left for work, but had no idea just how serious things had gotten. He could tell Marleigh was afraid and he knew he had to do something. "I will do the interview. You call that wanker and tell him to meet us at the park where he had seen us before. Get me some other clothes and we will have the portrait with us when we meet him. We can tell him that the portrait is a reproduction. He already knows you purchased it at a yard sale."

"But you don't have a green card." Marleigh looked worried.

"I shall tell him that I am an actor who was playing the part of Winston Spencer in a movie," Winston replied. "You said that there were reenactments going on here in Washington and I saw a news brief about a movie being filmed here about WW1. That would be the perfect alibi."

"What if he asks your real name and wants to see some identification?" Marleigh insisted, sounding worried.

"Well then, I will walk away from both of you in a huff, go behind a tree, and promptly disappear." Winston laughed. "He won't know where I am. I will be back in the portrait."

"I don't know, Winston..." She shook her head.

"We will just have to be in the right position. If he tries to follow me, you stop him and try to reason with him. When I walk far enough away from the portrait, I will be sucked back in and he shall be none the wiser."

"What if he asks why I bought the portrait?" Marleigh asked.

"That will be easy," Winston reassured her. "You saw it and could not believe the resemblance. You had seen me while the film was being made. I will be dressed in different clothes and comb my hair another way. I am serious in the portrait, but I will give him a big smile and look a bit goofy while I am at it."

"I hope that'll be enough," Marleigh said, unconvinced as she tried to hide her smile at the goofy part.

"It will have to be." Winston shrugged. "What is the alternative? He is not crazy enough to believe that the portrait and I are the same, is he?"

WINSTON INSTRUCTED Marleigh to wait two days before calling Jett Graham. He had her check on the location to make sure the movie was still being filmed. Maybe Jett Graham could be fooled. In any case this would be their only chance.

Winston had been watching the history channel and you tube on World War 1 in order to gather the information he felt he needed to convince Jett if he began asking questions about his role.

She had taken Friday off, the day they would meet him in the park and he hoped she wouldn't get in trouble on her job because of all this. Marleigh set the appointment with Jett at noon, but Winston didn't trust him. He told Marleigh they needed to leave at least two hours early to scour the perimeter.

They arrived at the park promptly at ten o'clock. The picnic table was still there of course. Marleigh had purchased him a pair of jeans and a tee shirt. He'd combed his hair back from his face and she'd even sprayed brown highlights in it. She sat the portrait by the bench and Winston sat on the table. He had Marleigh measure the distance from the table to different trees to determine which one he could walk to in order to be drawn back into the portrait. He already knew that Six yards was as far as he could go before disappearing. There were two trees in two different directions that would work marvelously.

He patted Marleigh's hand because he could see she was nervous. "This is going to work," he said soothingly to her. "Just wait and see."

"I hope you're right," Marleigh replied, looking up as a car door slammed. Both of them watched as Jett Graham approached.

"I told you he'd be early." Winston smiled hugely. "I understand you've been looking for me," he said approaching Jett while counting his steps.

"Yes, that's right," Jett said shaking his hand. "I know I'm early. How long have you two been here?"

"We just arrived," Winston smoothly replied.

Jett kept looking around.

"Marleigh had to pick me up."

"Where do you live, and is your name really Winston Spencer?" Jett asked.

Winston sat back on the table and smiled. "I was part of a movie being filmed on 14th Street. That was why I was dressed in uniform, playing the part of a soldier. Of course, I'm not the real Winston Spencer."

"But there's an uncanny resemblance, don't you see?" Marleigh asked picking up the portrait and holding it up next to Winston.

Jett looked at the portrait and then back at Winston. "Yes, I can see there are some similarities. Are you kin to the Spencers?"

"Heavens no!" Winston exclaimed. "I'm just playing the part."

"So, are you here on a visa?" Jett insisted.

"I'm an American," Winston lied.

"Really? Why the accent?" Jett asked suspiciously.

"I'm playing a part after all," Winston explained. "Did you like my acting as I stood on the table fencing? Did my accent sound authentic?"

"Is that what you were doing?" Jett asked in disbelief, "Acting...You were acting."

"Exactly." Winston nodded.

"Then why did you run off before? What did you have to hide?" Jett insisted.

"I was trying to get to know Marleigh better, and you ruined it," Winston accused while wiggling his brows at Jett. "That wasn't very sporting of you, my boy. There was nothing further for me to do but to leave. You rained on my parade."

"Do you have any identification on you now, confirming that you're a US citizen," Jett insisted. "What is your real name?"

Winston jumped up from the table. "You sir, are an arse! What is it with you? Are you from Immigration? Who are you to demand my identification?"

"If you have nothing to hide—" Jett began.

"I have nothing to prove either...at least not to the likes of you," Winston interrupted him while looking angry. He turned to Marleigh, speaking loudly, "I should never have let you convince me to come here and meet this oaf." He then stalked off in a huff.

Jett attempted to follow him but Marleigh quickly blocked his way.

"See what you've done? You've pissed him off. I still expect you to keep your end of the bargain," she insisted, hindering his pursuit of Winston.

"I know what I told you," he snapped walking around her. He looked around and saw that Winston had disappeared. "Where did he go?"

"How should I know?" Marleigh placed her hands on her hips. "My back was to him when he walked off."

"How did you find him?" Jett insisted. "Where did he come from?"

"The movie was still being filmed two days ago, so I went down there and luckily, I spotted him. I don't know where he is now because the film has wrapped up."

"Where did you pick him up at in order to bring him here?" Jett persisted with his questions.

"At the Walmart on 1st Street, North West," Marleigh lied.

Jett cursed under his breath. "I suppose you don't have any information on him that you can give me?"

"No. I thought you'd get all your information from him today."

"Something's not right," Jett insisted. "One minute he's here and the next minute he's gone! You've got to get in touch with him again."

"And exactly how am I supposed to do that?" Marleigh asked. "I only found him because the movie was still being filmed. It's over now."

"How did you meet him to begin with?" Jett snapped. "Something's not right with your story."

"I went down to watch the filming and I spotted him. He looked just like my painting. I hung around and waited until I could get his attention and then I told him about it. He asked to see it, so we met up in the park. That was the same day you found us."

"How did he get here?" Jett snapped angrily.

"How the hell should I know?" Marleigh said throwing up her hands. "He told me to meet him with the painting, and I did."

"So you just met up with this complete stranger in a park," Jett asked, unconvinced.

"He was an actor and he was really cute," Marleigh said laughing.

"Women." Jett groaned, shaking his head. "I'll have to get in touch with the production company and see if I can get his name from them."

"Good luck with that," Marleigh said grinning as she picked up the portrait and headed back to her car.

Chapter Fifteen

JETT GRAHAM WAS FURIOUS. How had this happened? He had the Winston Spencer lookalike right there in front of him, and he now knew nothing more than he had before the interview. Something wasn't right.

Still, he had to admit that whatever was going on, most likely Marleigh wasn't a part of it. She'd been there with her back to him when the actor had walked off in a huff. She couldn't have aided his escape.

He had even followed her home, but she hadn't made any stops. She went straight to her apartment taking the portrait with her. He sat there for hours but she never came back out.

Then he'd found the production company filming the movie and was informed that no actor matching his description had ever been on the payroll, nor was there even a part in the movie for a British actor named Winston Spencer. He'd been duped, and for some reason this so-called actor had lied to him as well as Marleigh.

His gut kept telling him Marleigh's portrait and this actor looking like Spencer was no accident. Being a freelancer, his time was his own, but he needed a story to pay the rent. He decided to contact Tim Hale and see what he knew and if there was some connection between this antique dealer and the bogus Winston Spencer. He'd obtained the addresses that the Wright woman had mailed the boxes off to. It pays to have contacts, and he had one at FedEx that had no problem looking up the information he wanted.

He pulled out his phone and texted Tim Hale to set up an interview. Maybe Tim would be willing to pay him for the information

he'd obtained, and he may even tell him about the portrait in Marleigh
Winter's possession if the price was right.

MARLEIGH GROANED AS she got into her car. She'd shown up at
Gertrude's at 7 am that morning and worked until 5 pm in order to pay
off her debt for the two remaining binders. She had placed them in the
trunk of her car, and was about to pull out.

Gertrude came out of the house while waving at her to stop.

"Is everything all right?" she asked rolling down her window.

"Yes dear," Gertrude replied. She handed her a yellowed piece of
vellum that looked ragged around the edges. "This fell out of one of the
binders when you were walking out."

"Thanks," Marleigh said taking it.

"You did good," Gertrude said. "I hope you enjoy your purchases."

"I will," Marleigh said laughing. She watched as the FedEx truck
pulled up. "Do you need me to stay?"

"Of course not." Gertrude smiled. She pointed to a car pulling up
behind the FedEx truck. "That's my husband now. We're going out to
dinner, so I told him to meet me here."

"Well you have fun," Marleigh said as she backed out of the driveway slowly.

Gertrude's husband got out of the car and waved.

She briefly waved back as she pulled onto the street.

The drive home seemed to take forever. Traffic was heavy and it was
raining. Marleigh felt glad when she pulled up in front of her apartment and slipped the paper Gertrude had given her into her purse. She
didn't want it to get wet. While she didn't have an umbrella, she did
have her raincoat. She slipped it on before grabbing the cloth bag con-
taining the remaining binders she'd placed in a trash bag to keep them
dry. She looked around, almost expecting Jett Graham to jump out at

her at any moment. The parking lot was full, but quiet. Maybe he was out chasing another story, though she doubted it.

She got out of the car and rushed to her apartment, letting herself in with her key. She took off the dripping rain coat, hung it by the door, then carried her purse and the plastic bag into the bedroom.

Winston was in his usual place on the wall and the television was on a commercial. She picked up the remote, cutting it off and called Winston from the painting. She sat her purse and the bag next to the bed.

"How was your day?" Winston asked smiling as he sat down his hat and sword. "No Jett Graham or Tim Hale, I hope."

"Nope. It was a good day," Marleigh said sitting on the bed and kicking off her sneakers. "Gertrude worked me like a government mule, but I now have the final two books. I'm exhausted, so you'll have to read them and fill me in. I think I'll sleep in tomorrow."

"You should," Winston agreed, sitting next to her. "You've worked hard today and I can see that you are in need of my services."

Marleigh groaned. "I don't think I'll be much fun tonight, Winston. My whole body aches."

"I'm talking about a rub down; not sex." Winston chuckled.

"That's just what the doctor ordered." Marleigh sighed.

She got undressed and before she went into the bathroom, she took Winston's portrait off of the wall and sat it by the door, leaving it open. "This way, you won't be sucked back in because I'm in the bathroom. You'll be fine as long as you stay on the bed."

"I'm not going anywhere," Winston replied stripping down to his underwear. "I'll be right here waiting for you."

Marleigh took a hot shower and grabbed the liniment out of the medicine cabinet. She came out of the bathroom naked, drying herself with a towel. Winston looked up at her from the bed, and she could see the desire in his eyes. If only she wasn't so tired.

"Come, lie on the bed," Winston invited, putting down one of the books he held in his hand. He patted the bed.

Marleigh moved closer and handed Winston the liniment, dropping the towel where she stood. She climbed on the bed and lay on her stomach. She groaned in delight as Winston began to massage her sore muscles. He had wonderful hands, with long fingers. He seemed to know just what she needed.

"You know that if you need anything else from me, I'm here," he whispered in her ear.

"I know."

He turned her over and continued, starting with her toes and working his way up her body.

Marleigh couldn't contain her groans of delight and lay there on the bed totally content when Winston had finished.

She watched him through half lidded eyes as he moved around the room, picking up her clothes and placing them in the hamper. His cock was semi erect and she felt warmth spread throughout her body. "You don't have to do that," she murmured, half asleep. If only she wasn't so tired!

"Nonsense," Winston responded. "Get some rest."

"There's a paper in my purse you should read," Marleigh said yawning. "Gertrude said that it fell out one of the books when I was carrying them to the car."

Winston came back over to her, leaning down kissing her lips softly. He then moved to her chest of drawers and held up a nightgown, inspecting it. He walked back to the bed, handing her the gown. "I'll handle it. You get some rest."

WINSTON WATCHED AS Marleigh drifted off to sleep. He walked over to her purse and opened it, finding the paper she'd told him about.

It turned out to be a piece of yellowed, high quality vellum with gilt lettering, he began to read it, and found a poem written there.

Bound eternally by blood,
The ties never die.
He remains youthful and strong,
Although useless and dry.
His world surrounds him eternally,
Mahogany, oak, pine & beech.
Freedom possible but elusive,
The lesson I teach.
Freedom rests in the Mahogany,
Possessing its love is the key,
Whose blood once was captured,
But now who is free.
In time the two will join,
The bonds quickly to fray.
And when together the words spoken,
The debt it will pay.
For the love is much stronger,
The one bound must be free.
So speak the words openly
To the Canuk and to me
By Temperance

Winston read the poem several times. He knew this was what they were looking for.

He hadn't expected a poem but he hadn't known what to expect. He decided not to wake Marleigh, but instead read the other two binders to see what they had to say.

JETT SAT IN THE RESTAURANT sipping his coffee. He glanced at his watch. Tim Hale would be arriving at any moment.

He'd secured a table facing the door and watched as the big, burly, Brit walked in and looked around. Spotting Jett, he headed towards him.

"Good morning," Jett said smiling.

Tim grunted and pulled out a chair. "Whatcha' have for me?"

"Ah, right to the point I see." Jett laughed. "I have the addresses where the books you wanted were shipped. How much are you willing to pay me for the information?"

"Five hundred, the same thing I told you in my text," Tim insisted. "Don't try to change that now. You agreed."

"Of course," Jett said. "Cash only."

"Of course," Tim said nodding as he pulled out the money. "Now give me the addresses and they better be right."

"Oh, they are," Jett insisted. "I have a contact who was able to go into the FedEx computer system." He handed the paper to Tim. "There were three boxes shipped to three different addresses."

"It'll take me a while to hunt these people down," Tim complained.

"I've also obtained their phone numbers," Jett said holding up another piece of paper. "For only one hundred dollars more, I'll give them to you."

"I can get that information myself," Tim grunted.

"Why do that work when I have it right here?" Jett waved the paper. "Surely, its worth another one hundred dollars."

Tim quickly peeled off another bill and threw it on the table. "Fine! Now what about the painting. Did you find out who has it?"

"Yes, I was able to obtain that information," Jett said eying him.

"I suppose you want more money?"

"Money or information," Jett said smoothly. "I met a man calling himself Winston Spencer. When I first met him, he was dressed exactly as the Winston Spencer in the painting."

Tim Hale's eyes grew big and then narrowed.

Jett continued knowing he had the man's full attention, "I was talk-ing to him, and he suddenly disappeared when I started questioning him. I met him the second time, but he wasn't in uniform. He refused to give me any identification or give me his real name. Then once again, he disappeared like magic. Poof! He was gone. I know that you think I'm crazy, but I discovered that he was never in the movie like he said. The production company had never heard of him."

"Was the painting nearby when you talked to him?" Tim asked.

"Yes, how did you know that?" Jett gasped.

Tim Hale didn't answer, but rubbed his jaw. "Who has the paint-ing?"

Jett didn't like giving information when he was being kept in the dark. He knew now that the painting and the actor were connected, but how? "That will cost you," he said crossing his arms.

"How much?" Tim grumbled.

"The truth," Jett replied simply.

WHEN MARLEIGH AWOKE, she glanced at her phone and saw it was almost eleven in the morning.

Winston sat on the floor, going through all four of the binders.

"Good morning," she said sitting up. "Don't tell me that you've been on the floor all night."

"No, you got up about 2 am and went in the bathroom shutting the door. Of course, since you'd hung the portrait back in its place, I was sucked in. Lucky for me though, you called for me before you crawled back into bed and pulled the cover over your head." He chuckled.

"Yeah, lucky for you."

"Of course," Winston continued, "When I came back, I was fully dressed once again and had to undress myself all over again."

"Such a bother," Marleigh said giggling.

"Yes, it can be a trial."

Marleigh quickly ran into the bathroom.

"Marleigh!" Winston called after her.

She laughed, knowing he would once again... have to undress. After a couple of minutes, she came out of the bathroom calling him.

He appeared standing by the bed. "You like torturing me, don't you?" he asked quirking a brow.

"Every now and then," she smirked, watching him undressing again.

"Maybe I won't tell you what I found," Winston said, folding his clothes.

"Now don't be like that," Marleigh replied, climbing on the bed and propping the pillows against the headboard. She leaned back and crossed her arms.

"Well, the paper that you had in your purse is the key," Winston began. "It's a poem by Temperance, and it's the key to my freedom, but I don't know what all of it means. I read the other two books and she talks about getting the portrait from my mother's estate, but nothing about the spell."

"There's nothing of value in the last two books?" Marleigh asked surprised.

"Oh, she talks about casting the spell, but not how it was done. She has entries on our interactions which I already know about. The last book mainly talked about her son who was a gambler who she had disowned."

"Isn't he the one who lost you to Miles, in a game of cards?"

"Exactly," Winston replied. "The last two books were no help at all, but this poem is the key."

"Read it to me," Marleigh insisted.

Winston picked up the vellum and sat on the bed by her. "Bound eternally by blood, the ties never to die; he remains youthful and strong, though useless and dry." He looked at Marleigh. "I think she's speaking about me."

"I think you're right, but you are far from useless or dry!" Marleigh laughed.

"Why, thank you my lady." Winston gave her a nod. "The world surrounds him eternally; mahogany, oak, pine and beech; freedom possible, but elusive, this lesson I teach." He paused to look at Marleigh. "I'm surrounded by trees? There are no trees."

"She's speaking of wood," Marleigh said excitedly. "She's talking about your picture frame."

"A frame isn't made of four different types of wood," Winston insisted. "That's highly unusual."

"Maybe it had to be because of the spell she was casting, keep reading."

"Freedom rests in the mahogany, possessing its love is the key; whose blood once was captured, but now who is free." He frowned. "I couldn't figure this part out. I read it over and over again. If she's talking about the frame, was it captured meaning the tree was cut down? If so, how can it now be free?" he glanced over at Marleigh who'd closed her eyes.

She opened them slowly. "It's a metaphor. She's no longer talking about a tree. She said that its blood was captured. Trees don't have blood. She's talking about a person... a black person, captured and now free."

Winston looked puzzled. "You were never captured."

"My people were captured, Winston. We came here as slaves."

"Of course! That explains this next part: 'In time the two will join, the bonds quickly to fray; and when together the words spoken, the debt it will pay. For love is much stronger, the one bound must be free; so speak the words openly to the Canuk and to me.'" He gazed back up at her while grinning. "Well we've joined together obviously. Remember when I told you that later, I felt a burden lift from me and I felt happier? This is what the poem is talking about! 'The bonds quickly to fray'!"

"The bonds on you from the spell are starting to fray," Marleigh said excitedly.

"Yes, I believe that that is what it's saying." Winston nodded. "Do you think we're onto something?"

"Yes, but what words must be spoken?" Marleigh asked. "And who the heck is Canuk? I don't know anyone by that name."

"Neither do I," he said replacing the poem with the binders. "But don't you see, we're on the right track. This proves that the spell can be broken."

"We still don't know how," Marleigh insisted. "But I bet you that man, Tim Hale knows. Why else would he be looking for the binders and for the painting? What if he tries to steal you from me?"

"If he knows anything about the spell or the history of it, then he'll know that stealing it is useless. The only way that it can change possession is for you to sell it or give it away. If he steals me, I'll come right back to you."

"That's good to know," Marleigh replied.

"Another one of Temperance's rules," Winston said. "I just remembered it. I wish she'd written them all down, but I didn't find them in the binders, so I'll just have to rely on my memory."

Chapter Sixteen

JETT GRAHAM COULDN'T wrap his head around the tall tale, Tim Hale just told him. What was this Brit really about? Did he really expect him to believe that the Winston Spencer he'd talked to, actually came from the painting? The man was one step short of being committed to the looney bin.

"I tell you, it's the truth and I need those binders and that painting," Tim insisted.

"Why? Why do you need them?" Jett asked. "Let's say I believe you. Why is this such a crisis?"

"Because," Tim explained patiently, "the painting once belonged to my great -grandmother. My grandfather lost it in a bet along with the binders. He hid that from his mother who was on an invalid and bedridden at the time. He didn't want to tell her what he'd done because she'd given them to him for safe keeping. My father told me that she found out before she died. She got better for a while and searched the house and couldn't find the painting or the binders. She confronted my grandfather and put a curse on him. His family line would cease unless he regained ownership of the painting and the binders. He already had a son and so he didn't care about the curse. Still, he was scared of his mum and tried to locate the man who had them."

"Well, if the curse was real..." Jett stared at him. "You wouldn't be here now. Your line should have ended with your father."

"Yeah, except my father had already gotten a girl pregnant at the age of 14," Tim explained. "He married my mum knowing that I would be the only child he had because of that blasted curse." He shook his head. "My great grandmother died at the age of a hundred and three in 1938. My grandfather searched all over England for the bloke, but never found him. All he knew was that he was named Miles McGregor. My father was the one who was able to trace him to a ship that sailed to America. He died last year, so now I'm here trying to break the curse on my family."

"That's some story," Jett replied in disbelief.

"It's the truth," Tim insisted. "Now I've told you everything and I'm going to hunt down that painting, because my grandfather told my father that the painting contained words that would break the curse on our family. I'm hoping that the location of the words was revealed in the binders, which is why I wanted copies."

"Let's say I believe you," Jett said eying him doubtfully. "How did Winston Spencer get out of the painting?"

"His owner has the power to call him forth," Tim explained. "However, he can't move more than a few feet from the painting, or he'll return to it."

Jett gasped in surprise. *So that was how she did it! The whole interview had been a sham! If Tim Hale was telling the truth, and he had no reason to lie, then Marleigh Winters knew that Winston Spencer would disappear.* They'd played him. He stared at Tim. "I know who has the painting and I bet that same person has those books if what you're telling me is true."

"They must have the binders; otherwise how would they know that he could leave the painting?"

"Exactly," Jett agreed, remembering how Marleigh had the painting with her both times when he talked to Winston. "Forget chasing down those addresses," he said grabbing the paper back and crumbling it up. "The owner of the portrait most likely knew that these people don't have the books. She would have kept them for herself. This was a wild goose chase."

"She?" Tim asked.

"I'll take you to her. It's Marleigh Winters and together, we can convince her to sell it to you. How much are you willing to pay?"

"I'll pay fifteen hundred dollars," Tim insisted. "After I get what I want, of course. You and your girl can decide how to split it between yourselves."

"Deal," Jett said standing. "Let's go."

MARLEIGH SAT AT HER laptop researching the word Canuk. She'd hidden the poem separately from the binders which were now on a shelf by her bed.

Winston sat next to her watching as she scanned the screen.

"Canuk is a slang term for a person from Canada," she said. "Do you know any Canadians?"

Winston shook his head. "Not really. Maybe we just have to say the words in front of someone that is a Canadian."

"What words could the poem be talking about?" Marleigh asked.

"Maybe it is something simple, like 'I love you,'" Winston speculated.

"I don't think that's it." Marleigh shook her head. "The poem also said that we have to say the words to this Canuk and to Temperance who is long gone. It sounds to me like whatever these words are will bring Temperance back even if it's temporary."

"You are probably right."

Marleigh closed the laptop. They'd been working on this the entire day and she was hungry. "I'm going out to get something to eat. Do you want me to bring you something back?"

"You know that I do not need to eat," Winston pointed out.

"I know, but I thought you might enjoy the taste of some food. There's a new British pub open across town. I could go there and bring you something back that reminds you of home."

"Really?" Winston asked. "Do they have kidney pie?"

"What?" Marleigh asked wrinkling her face in disgust. "Kidney pie? Sounds gross!"

"It's quite tasty," Winston insisted. "Remember, you told me that you eat pigs' feet."

"Pigs feet are good," Marleigh replied. "I like pigs' feet."

"I like kidney pie," Winston insisted. "I'll taste your pigs' feet, if you taste my kidney pie."

"I'd have to stop twice at two different restaurants in order to buy both kidney pie and pigs feet," Marleigh replied. "I'll take your word for it. Maybe I can find something at the British Pub Restaurant that I'll like."

"Try fish and chips," Winston suggested.

Marleigh picked up her purse, gave him a quick kiss, and walked out of the room.

WINSTON COULD HEAR someone banging on the front door and ringing the doorbell. Everything was quiet because Marleigh hadn't left the telly on.

In a few moments, he heard someone at the window trying to open it.

He watched helplessly as the window was pried open and a young teenage boy climbed into the bedroom.

The teen looked around and then his eyes fell on Winston. The boy went back to the window. "I see it," he said to someone Winston couldn't see.

"Take it down, boy and I'll pay you that hundred dollars I promised," a voice said from outside.

The boy turned back to Winston and took him off the wall. He was scraped against the windowsill as the boy handed him out the window. Winston looked at the man who held him.

He was over fifty, tall with salt and pepper unruly curls. He grinned, revealing perfectly white teeth. "Here ya go," the man said to the skinny thief. "Don't spend it all in one place." He put Winston in his car and he lay the painting on its side, and

Winston now hoped the man would be gone by the time Marleigh got back with the food.

"Here are those old books you asked me to look for," he heard the thief say. "There was two of them on the shelf by the bed."

"Is that all of them?" the big man demanded.

"That's all I saw," the thief responded.

"Good. Now be gone," the man said as he got in the car.

Winston felt the car pull away from the apartment. They hadn't gone more than a mile when he found himself back on the wall in Marleigh's apartment.

The thief had left the window open in the bedroom, and he prayed she would return soon. Obviously, the man who'd stolen him must have been Tim Hale. Winston could tell by his cockney accent. Apparently, Mr. Hale didn't realize that because of the spell, he couldn't be stolen, at least not for long. He hoped Hale didn't know this rule, and wouldn't return.

An hour later, he heard a key in the front door and knew Marleigh was back.

"I got your kidney pie," she yelled from the kitchen.

He heard her come down the hall and open the bedroom door.

Immediately, she noticed the open window. "What the hell?" She turned to Winston and called him out of the painting. "What happened here?" She looked at the shelf. "Two of the binders! They're gone!"

"I know," Winston said walking over to her. "A young boy came through the window and took me off the wall and gave me to a man speaking cockney. He was big with black hair mixed with gray."

"Tim Hale!"

"Yes, and apparently he doesn't know that he can't steal me." Winston felt worried. "I hope he doesn't come back here."

Marleigh shut the window. "I forgot to put the alarm on. That won't happen again. "He took two books from the shelf, but the other two are still in the bag. How did he know that I'm your owner unless that asshole, Jett Graham told him?"

Winston shook his head, knowing that most likely Jett had told him.

"Maybe we can use his ignorance to our advantage." Marleigh suggested as she took down the portrait. "I'll hide you and if he does double back, he will see that you're still missing."

Winston nodded. "You can tell Jett Graham that someone stole me and see what he has to say about it. We have to be careful though. Those two may be working together."

Marleigh nodded and rummaged through her purse for her phone. "I'm calling him right now. We don't have all the binders, but we don't need them. Thank God, I kept the poem separate from them."

JETT LOOKED AT HIS phone and was surprised to see Marleigh calling him. "Well... well...well... Miss Winters. To what do I owe this pleasure," he drawled.

"Someone stole my painting off the wall."

"Stole the painting!" Jett gasped. "When?"

"I went out to get something to eat and when I came back, the window was open and the painting was gone."

Jett knew Tim Hale must have taken it, the double crosser. Tim agreed that Jett would get it and in turn, Tim would pay him the fifteen hundred dollars. Instead, it appeared that Tim had taken matters into his own hands and stole it. He'd convinced Jett to meet up with him in an hour. Jett had wanted to go over to Marleigh's apartment immediately after they left the restaurant, but Tim had insisted that he had another appointment that he had to take care of first. "Have you called the cops?" Jett asked.

"No, not yet," Marleigh replied. "I'm giving you a chance to return it. You're going to be the number one suspect!"

"I didn't steal it," Jett protested. "Why would I do that?"

"You knew that I had it, and that Hale wanted it. He didn't know that the portrait or the binders were in my possession. Now two of the binders and the painting have been stolen!"

Jett's mind went into overdrive. He didn't need the cops hauling him downtown for questioning. He had to find Hale.

"How much did he offer you to steal it?" Marleigh asked angrily.

"I didn't steal it," Jett insisted. "Maybe he figured it out. He's been to your apartment before. I told you about it, remember?"

"Yes, I remember. I'm sure he offered you top dollar to get the portrait and I think you're lying. You stole it."

Jett could feel his blood begin to boil. "You lied to me!" he accused. "You set me up, had me thinking that I was crazy when your so called 'actor' just vanished into thin air. Tim Hale told me that he's the same man in the portrait, and that you had the power to make him come alive! You knew Winston Spencer would disappear as soon as he walked away from me! You played me!"

"Do you think the cops are going to believe that story?" Marleigh asked sweetly.

"I didn't take the damn painting!" Jett insisted loudly. "He promised me fifteen hundred dollars to tell him who had it. I didn't know he was going to steal it!"

"What did you expect him to do?" Marleigh snapped. "He's shady and you are too!"

"His story sounded crazy, but it did explain how Winston Spencer disappeared." He tried to remain calm. "We can work together...try to get him back. I know where Hale is staying and I have his cell number. Don't call the cops."

Marleigh grew quiet on the other end of the line.

He hoped she was considering what he said. "Look," he pleaded, "Don't call the cops. If I can help you get your portrait back, then I'll leave here and return to my own country."

"Your own country?" Marleigh asked.

"Yes, I'm Canadian and my work visa is about to expire."

"Wow, look at the pot calling the kettle black!" Marleigh laughed. "You're looking for illegal aliens and you see one in the mirror every day."

'It's just work, nothing personal," Jett grumbled. "Do we have a deal?"

"Meet me at the park," Marleigh said, then she ended the call.

Chapter Seventeen

"YOU CANNOT MEET THAT wanker!" Winston protested. "Not alone!"

"I have no choice," Marleigh replied calmly. "I can't take you with me. You're stolen, remember? He won't hurt me. He's stupid.... but harmless."

"Never underestimate your enemy," Winston insisted.

"Right...but he's a Canadian," Marleigh reminded him. "He's the Canuk. We need him. We just have to keep him in the dark until we can figure out what the words are that we need to say in front of him that will bring Temperance back and break the curse."

"What about Tim Hale?" Winston asked. "I think it's only a matter of time before he figures out that the curse won't allow me to be stolen. He'll come back here, and then what? There's no telling what a desperate man will do."

"Which is why I have to meet up with Jett," Marleigh insisted. "Maybe Hale told him something that we could use. After all, he did tell Jett about the spell."

"I cannot believe Hale would ever spill his guts like that," Winston said shaking his head.

Marleigh glanced down at her phone. "I'm meeting Jett in thirty minutes, so I have to go."

Winston watched as she slid the painting under the bed. "Not a very good hiding place," he pointed out.

"That's the best I can do for now. I can only hope that he doesn't come back here, and if he does, he'll see that you're not on the wall. I'll leave the blinds open just in case."

"Be careful," Winston said kissing her.

"I will," she promised.

JETT PACED BACK AND forth nervously as he waited for Marleigh to come. He sat on the picnic table, then jumped up and walked around it several times.

He'd called Tim Hale on his cell, but it went straight to voicemail. More than likely, he was on his way back to England. What a fool he'd been to trust him.

If Marleigh called the cops, they'd soon discover that his visa was about to expire and most likely ship him back to his hometown of Nelson, in British Columbia Canada. He didn't want to go back there. He had to fix this!

He heard her when she pulled up and watched her park her car. He had to convince her that the two of them could work together and get the painting back.

"Look, I didn't steal your painting," he began as she approached.

"Save it," she snapped. "You're the reason we're in this mess. You ran your mouth, expecting payment and now it's blown up in your face."

"I tried to call him, but it goes to voicemail," Jett explained. "We can go by his place, try to reason with him."

"He's probably long gone by now," Marleigh pointed out, sitting at the table.

"Is it true? Did Winston Spencer come out of the painting?"

"Maybe," Marleigh hedged.

"How did you do it?" Jett asked anxiously. "How did you know you could call him out? Is he like a genie and a slave to whoever possesses him?"

"This is not an interview, Jett," she retorted. "Shut up."

He grew quiet for a moment.

"Look, what did he tell you about the portrait?" she said, turning to him. "Don't lie to me either!"

"He said that his great-grandmother owned the portrait and that his grandfather lost it in a card game. His grandfather was able to hide it from his mother because she was bedridden and sick. Then she got better and discovered the painting was gone. He said his father overheard them arguing and his grandmother said that the owner of the portrait could call the man in the portrait from the painting like a genie from a lamp and that he would do whatever the owner told him to. His father told him that his grandfather didn't believe what she was telling him, but Hale does, because he knew that his great grandmother was a witch. He also said she put a curse on her son and his entire line because of what he did and the only way to break the curse was to get the portrait and those books back."

"What kind of curse?" Marleigh asked.

"Their family line would end, but his father already had a son and grandson on the way, so the curse would only affect him and he wants to break it." Desperately, he grabbed Marleigh's hand. "I've told you everything. We can hunt him down ourselves. I have the resources. Don't call the cops and have me deported."

Marleigh snatched her hand back. "I'd be a fool to trust you."

Jett sighed. "I know, but you have all the cards now."

"That's true," Marleigh replied, grinning.

MARLEIGH FOLLOWED JETT to the Super 8 Motel where Tim Hale had been staying.

After Jett went in and talked to the clerk, he came back looking dejected. "He checked out this morning."

"I figured as much," Marleigh replied.

"Now what?" Jett asked.

Marleigh knew she needed Jett in order to break the spell, but she'd decided to tell him as little as possible in advance. She asked him to follow her back to her apartment. She then would call Winston forth and then see if they could figure out how to break the spell. If he bailed on her, no one would believe his story anyway and he would be deported when she filed a police report on the breaking and entering.

She parked and waited for him to get out of the car.

He rushed over to her, looking puzzled. "Why are we coming back here to your place?"

"You'll see," she replied. "We need to strategize and figure out our next steps."

"Of course." Jett nodded, though he looked very curious.

As she put the key in the lock, she heard Jett gasp. She looked up to see Tim Hale with his arm around Jett's neck with a gun pointed at his head. "Open the door," he hissed. "Now!"

Marleigh opened the door.

Hale pushed them both in and slammed it shut. "Now, where is my painting!" he demanded.

"Someone stole it off my wall," Marleigh snapped angrily. "Someone broke in and stole it."

"I told her that I didn't take it," Jett insisted.

"I took it," Tim said smugly. "Now someone has taken it from my car, and I figure it has to be one of you." He looked around and pushed the muzzle of his gun to her back. "Move. We're going to your bedroom." He motioned to Jett who followed her back to the bedroom.

Marleigh opened the door, turning to Hale and Jett. "As you can see," she said pointing to the wall. "My painting is missing. I couldn't have stolen it back because I had no idea where it was. I thought Jett had taken it because he was the only one I could think of who'd knew that I had it."

"Sit on the bed!" Tim ordered while looking around. "Yeah, I stole it. I know you couldn't have taken it. When I stopped at the gas station to use the facilities, I came back and found the painting gone even though my car was locked." He waved the gun at Jett. "The only one who could have taken it was YOU. I bet you figured out that I wasn't going to pay you. You probably followed me here, saw me nab the painting and followed me. You took your chance when I made that stop, but that was a fatal mistake. I want what is mine."

"I don't have it!" Jett insisted.

"I could blow your head off right now," Tim hissed, smacking him with the gun.

Blood began to pour from Jett's temple.

Marleigh screamed. "There's no need for this!" she cried. "He can't lead you to the portrait if you kill him!" Panicked, she jumped up and grabbed a towel from the chair that she'd used that morning.

"You sit down," Tim insisted, rubbing his hand across his face, waving the gun.

Marleigh could tell Tim was trying to figure out what to do next. She decided to try to distract him and at the right moment, she could call Winston forth and he would attack. She knew he could hear the conversation from under the bed. "Why do you want the painting?" she asked.

"It belonged to my family!" Tim insisted. "Until my fool grand pappy lost it in a card game. My real name is Tim Rice, not Hale. I used a fake name so that you wouldn't make the connection before I wanted you to."

"He needs to break the curse, so that his line won't end," Jett said as she handed him the towel.

Tim laughed. "There is no family curse. I made that up." He waved the gun around some more. "However, there are one hundred gold sovereigns in there with Mr. Spencer. One hundred gold sovereigns from the nineteenth century. Do you know how much they're worth today?

More than a hundred thousand dollars! Even more, if I auction them off. Granny was a sly one. Her brother was a Spencer, the boy in the paintings' father in fact. My granny was the daughter of Spencer's mistress whose mum died when she was just thirteen. Of course, her big brother, the toff's son provided for her. He gave her that money over the years and she kept it, hid it in fact. Because my grandfather was a gambler, she hid them in the portrait when she cast that spell on it. My grandfather never believed she was a witch, but my father did. I guess Granny didn't expect him to gamble off the portrait." He pointed the gun at Jett. "Now, I'm losing my patience, so tell me where it is!"

"How are you going to get the money if it's in the painting?" Marleigh asked.

"I still have to figure that out," Tim admitted.

"I know the words to call him out of the painting," Marleigh said.

"How did you know that?" Tim asked suspiciously.

"His name was on the back of the portrait," Marleigh replied. She wasn't about to tell him about the dream. She had to keep him distracted and let him think he was still in control.

"I figured the words were on the back of the painting," Tim said as he stared at her. "My father said the key was with the painting in the frame, but now I realize that it must be on the back."

Marleigh tried not to look surprised. *In the frame? The key was in the frame itself?* "Why did your father think it's in the actual frame?"

"Granny wrote a poem, but it's not in the books that you bought, it seems. My dad said the poem named the wood of the frame; oak, pine and beech. That's what the picture frame is made of, and that's what keeps him trapped in there. Pappy said that the key is in the wood somewhere which is why I need that painting and the poem to get my money."

"I don't have it, I tell you!" Jett insisted, holding the towel against his head.

"We are going to leave here and go to your place," Tim insisted. "If I don't get my painting, I'm killing you both there and leaving the gun so the cops will think that it was a murder suicide. I'm broke and I have nothing to lose. And I want that gold. Now get up!" He grabbed Jett by the neck with his beefy hand.

Marleigh jumped up. "Winston, please come forth," she whispered, hoping he would hear her.

Winston appeared and quickly drew his sword.

Tim's back was to him as he choked Jett.

Winston swiftly stabbed him in the back, and slashed his arm so he would release Jett.

The gun flew from his other hand and landed on the floor. "What the hell?" Tim yelled, falling forward on the bed. He then flipped over.

Jett jumped off the bed coughing. He was bleeding, but it didn't stop him from attempting to get the gun.

However, Marleigh quickly picked it up. She'd never held a gun in her life, but she pointed it at Tim's head.

Winston then placed the tip of his sword at Tim's throat. "I should kill you," he growled.

"How did you get here?" Tim asked, holding his arm. "You almost killed me!"

"The one in your back is a flesh wound, and no major artery has been severed in your arm," Winston pointed out. "You will live." He pushed the tip of the blade in a bit, drawing blood. "However, the right cut to the throat can end you right here, right now."

"Don't!" Tim pleaded. "Where's the painting? Where'd you come from?"

"When Temperance cast the spell, she made a provision. I could never be stolen. I could only be sold or given away freely. Apparently, she made a bad choice taking me to her son's home when she became ill. She gave me to him, believing he thought that I was worthless, and wouldn't sell me. I don't think she considered he would actually take me to a card game as collateral. That is how your family lost me to Miles. When he died, his daughter Gertrude sold me and I now belong to Marleigh until she gets rid of me."

"And that'll never happen," Marleigh said smiling.

Winston glanced over at Jett. "Now, it seems that your bleeding is under control, so we need to get rid of this riff raff."

"What do you want me to do?" Jett asked.

"Those gold sovereigns are mine!" Tim exclaimed. "I want what's mine."

"Actually, they belong to Miss Winters," Winston pointed out.

"My grandfather had the option to get those binders and that painting back in ninety days!" Tim exclaimed. "That bloke Miles left the country in thirty! He didn't hold up his end of the bargain."

"Exactly how do you expect Winston to get the gold?" She turned to Winston. "Did you recall seeing gold?"

"No, but I wasn't looking for it either," Winston admitted.

"It's there!" Tim insisted. "You just need to go back in there and get it."

"You have no authority here." Winston still held the tip of his sword at Tim's throat. He pressed it slightly, drawing blood once again. He glanced at Jett. "Get something to tie this fool up."

Jett jumped up and dropped the towel. His head had stopped bleeding, but the cut looked ugly.

"I have some rope I used when I moved here. In the kitchen, in a drawer," Marleigh urged. "Jett, go get it."

Jett left the room, returning with the rope. He tied Tim's hands behind his back.

"Sit!" Winston demanded, pushing Tim towards the chair. He turned to Marleigh. "Get the painting."

Marleigh reached under the bed, pulled it out, and leaned the portrait against the bed.

"Now, keep the gun on him and I'll go back. Call me out in five minutes. Keep an eye on both of them. I don't trust them, and you shouldn't either."

Marleigh nodded.

Winston walked out of the bedroom, so he would be drawn back into the portrait.

She turned to Jett. "Set your phone alarm for five minutes."

"Look, I'll leave. Forget about the money," Tim said while standing. "Just untie me and I'll go."

"Sit down," Marleigh hissed, "before I shoot you in the foot."

Tim sat back down on the bed.

She could tell he was planning his escape. The gun felt slick in her hand from her own sweat and she tried not to show him she was scared out of her mind. She glanced at Jett who kept watching her. She didn't trust him either and wished those five minutes was up already.

Before she knew what was happening, Tim jumped up and threw his weight at her, knocking her down. The gun flew from her hand and sailed across the room.

"Get the gun!" Rice yelled at Jett. "I'll split the gold with you when he brings it out."

Jett quickly picked up the gun and looked over at Marleigh to see if she was all right.

"Now untie me!" Tim demanded.

"No, you'll kill us both," Jett replied pointing the gun at him.

"I'll split the gold with you. I give you my word," Tim shouted angrily. "Untie me!"

"Are you okay, Marleigh?" Jett asked.

She sat up and rubbed her head. "I'm good," she responded as she stood up on shaky legs.

"Time's up then," Jett announced. "Call him back."

"Winston, come forth," Marleigh called out.

Winston appeared. He strode angrily across the room and punched Tim, square in the face. "You blighter!"

"Winston, I'm fine," Marleigh insisted grabbing his free hand.

"I ought to kill you," Winston seethed while placing his sword down onto Tim's throat, as the man lay sprawled on the bed. He looked over at Jett. "We need to get him out of here and make sure that he never returns."

"Did you find the money?" Marleigh asked.

"Yes, I had been sitting on it the whole time. It was in the chair cushion." He reached into his bearskin hat and pulled out a small sack.

"That gold is mine!" Tim shouted from his position on the bed.

"I tell you what," Marleigh said. "I don't believe you're totally broke, otherwise how would you get back home? Therefore, because I'm a nice person, I'll give you a portion of the gold—"

"But all of it belongs to me," Tim cut her off.

"No, actually all of it belongs to me," she pointed out. She glanced at Jett. "Thanks for the help earlier. Now, I know you aren't all bad."

"You're welcome," he said grinning. "I think?"

"I know you have contacts all around," Marleigh continued. "So, I'm going to give you ten of these," she said reaching into the bag and holding up a few of the coins. She then dropped them back in the bag. "You will take him to the airport and put him on a plane. I'm sure there's a ticket somewhere in his car since he checked out of his room." She turned to Tim. "And you will go willingly, now won't you."

"Of course," Tim answered with a grin.

"He's lying, of course," Marleigh stated with a shrug while looking at Winston. Then she glanced back over at Tim. "However, I know the remaining ninety pieces of gold means a lot to you, and I'd hate to turn them over to the police where you'd never see them again."

Tim glared at her. "You wouldn't do that! You want them for yourself!"

"I don't want it at all," Marleigh defended. "Look how much trouble it has caused me! No, I will box it up and FedEx it to you in England. Just leave me your address. I'll ship it and it'll be there in three days tops. Of course, the cost of shipping it will be taken into consideration."

"What do you mean exactly?" Rice asked as Jett forced him to stand.

"What I mean is that I'll ship the coins to you one at a time and you should have them all in ninety days... or so. Same amount of time your grandfather had, remember?"

"You bitch!" he snarled.

"Tut tut," she said walking over to him and slapping him hard. "That is for knocking me down. Now you," she said looking at Jett. "Will cover the cost of shipping them one at a time for the next ninety days."

"What?" Jett asked surprised. "I can't send a FedEx package each day for ninety days!"

"But you will because that's the only way you'll get your ten coins," Marleigh said. "According to Mr. Rice, each coin is valued at over six hundred dollars in US currency. That's six thousand dollars at least. I don't think it's too much to ask. Bring me ninety receipts and you'll get the coins. After all your scheming and trouble making, you're lucky to get anything."

"Fine." Jett sighed, admitting defeat. "We'll do this your way."

Marleigh nodded. "Now, let's get him ready to take his trip home. Then we'll escort our friend out of here. I'm sure his car is a rental, most likely from the airport." She pointed her finger at Tim. "Any funny business and the coins go back into the painting. So, I suggest you get on the very next plane going across the pond."

"Fine, I'll go." Rice sneered at her. "But I'll be back if you don't give me what's mine."

Winston looked proud of her as he gave her a nod.

"You don't have to worry about that..." Marleigh stared at Tim. "Because I never want to see your ugly face again."

Chapter Eighteen

MARLEIGH SENT JETT to search Tim's car while Winston changed his clothes.

The car in fact, was a rental and Jett located his ticket back to England in Rice's carry-on luggage. He was to leave that very night, returning to London. Marleigh could only conclude that he figured he'd have the portrait by then.

She wrapped his wounds in bandages and had Tim change his shirt from the clothes in his carryon bag. She then untied him.

Jett now had the gun on Tim and he told Marleigh that he knew how to use it.

Marleigh put the portrait in the front seat of the rental while Winston and Tim sat in the back.

Winston kept his sword pointed at Tim's throat.

"Be careful with that thing," Tim whined. "She could hit a bump and you'd slit my throat."

"Ah, well you better not drive too fast then, Marleigh." Winston grinned. "I would hate to get blood in this rental. Didn't you say that could incur additional charges?"

"That's right." Marleigh nodded. "So, you'd better behave Mr. Rice."

"Of course," Tim said as he stared out the window.

They arrived at the airport and Jett walked with Rice to turn in the rental car.

Marleigh stayed by Jett's car where Winston was now leaning on the hood. The portrait had been removed from the rental and placed inside.

After a bit, the two men returned from the rental booth.

"From this point, you're on your own, Mr. Rice," Marleigh stated. "I trust you will behave if you want that gold."

"I know," Tim grumbled, picking up his bags.

Jett said nothing as he pulled out a brown paper bag, removed the gloves he wore and put them inside. He then walked to a nearby garbage can and tossed it in.

Marleigh realized Jett had just gotten rid of the gun.

"Have a safe trip," Jett said nodding at Tim.

The three of them then got into the car and took off, leaving Tim staring after them.

"Do you think he'll behave?" Winston asked doubtfully. "What'll keep him from doubling back?"

"I took the few pounds he had left in his bag," Jett admitted. "He now only has his ticket and very little money. If he misses his flight, then he's stuck here. He won't be able to get another ticket. I took his credit card too, just in case."

Marleigh laughed. "You're such a scoundrel."

THE THREE OF THEM RETURNED to the apartment and sat Winston's portrait down in the living room.

"The bedroom's a mess!" Marleigh sighed. "We'll have to figure this out here."

"Figure what out?" Jett asked.

"How to break the spell so that Winston doesn't have to go back," Marleigh explained.

"Is that even possible?" Jett asked. "You don't have that poem that Rice said that you needed in order to break the spell."

"I have it," Marleigh admitted. She looked over at Winston. "I'll have to take the frame apart in order to search it for the key. Will that hurt you?"

"I do not know," Winston admitted, looking worried.

Marleigh looked at each corner of the painting. The frame was gold and she could see that the four corners were neatly fitted together. There appeared to be thick metal staples on back, attaching the portrait to the frame. "I'll have to remove the portrait from the frame itself." She gave Winston a concerned look. She then gently plied the large metal staples from the back of the portrait to loosen it from the frame. She glanced at Winston again, who lay on his back on the floor with his eyes closed.

"Are you all right," she asked nervously.

"Just a little dizzy," he replied. "Continue."

Marleigh carefully pried a few more of the staples.

Jett gently made a little pile of them on the floor.

When they were all removed, she jumped when she heard Winston groan. "Winston!"

"I'm fine," he reassured her. "My stomach is now a little queasy."

Marleigh cautiously took the portrait and laid it aside after separating it from the frame. "We can stop any time you say so."

"What's happening to him?" Jett asked, as he too, looked concerned.

"I think this is affecting him somehow," Marleigh answered with her best guess.

"Look carefully at each corner where the wood meets," Winston instructed, not moving.

Marleigh did as he said. She couldn't see anything from the front, but from the back, she could see that each part of the frame was indeed made from different types of wood. "There's a magnifying glass in my night stand." She glanced over at Jett. "Get it for me."

He quickly got up and returned with the glass.

She took it and peered closely at each corner of the frame. She gasped at what she discovered. In each corner, she could see something wedged between the fittings in all four corners. It looked like small pieces of paper. "There's tweezers in my purse, Jett. I have a manicure set. Bring it to me, please."

Jett rushed over to get her purse, then came back and handed it to her.

She took out a gold case. Opening it, she grabbed the tweezers. "Hold the magnifying glass while I carefully try to pull out what's stuck in there," she instructed.

Jett held the glass, paused and glanced up at Winston.

"Do it," he said from the floor.

Marleigh returned her attention to the frame. The last thing she wanted to do was to damage the wood or the small piece of paper wedged inside. She grabbed two sides of the frame, gently pulling them apart and the pressure created a small crack. Winston groaned, so she hurried as she used the tweezers and latched onto the bit of paper. She wiggled it back and forth until she could see it coming out. "I got it," she said triumphantly while holding it up. Cautiously, she placed the small piece of folded paper onto the floor.

Working carefully, she did the same thing with the other three sides until she had four small pieces of folded paper. "I got them, Winston," she said excitedly.

"Good," he whispered while still lying there with his eyes closed.

"Are you in pain?"

"A little, but read what is on the papers if you can," he instructed.

Marleigh carefully unfolded each piece of paper, each of them was no larger than an inch in diameter and two inches in length. The writing looked tiny, but legible. Each piece was numbered, followed by what appeared to be a bible scripture.

"There are scriptures written on each of the papers," Marleigh exclaimed. "Can you sit up, Winston?"

"I don't think so," he replied. "I still feel dizzy."

"I'll help you." Jett helped Winston to a sitting position and looked to Marleigh. "Now what?"

"I'll get my bible and read the scriptures in the presence of the Canuk, that's you Jett and then see what happens."

"No, we have to read them together," Winston reminded her.

"You're right." Marleigh nodded. "I'll look up each scripture and then print them out from my laptop in the order that's been instructed. Jett, can you bring me my laptop from the bedroom? I can't leave Winston," she explained. "My bible is on the nightstand."

Jett rushed back to her bedroom and brought the bible to her and her laptop.

It only took Marleigh a few minutes to type out the scriptures and print them.

"What do I have to do?" Jett asked.

"You just listen and we'll see what happens," Marleigh instructed. She came over to Winston and sat down beside him, handing him the scriptures that she'd printed twice. "We have to read these together. I used large print," she said looking at Winston. "Are you ready?"

"Yes," he responded.

They began to read together.

"Romans 12:21: Do not be overcome by evil, but overcome evil with good."

"Mark 4:22: For there is nothing hidden which will not be revealed, nor has anything been kept secret but that it should come to light."

"1 Peter 4:8, And above all things, have fervent love for one another, for love will cover a multitude of sins."

"John 8:36: So, if the son sets you free, you are free indeed."

WINSTON LOOKED AROUND the room, but there was no Temperance in sight. He felt better and was no longer dizzy, but something wasn't quite right. "I feel fine, but I don't think the spell is broken." He looked over at Marleigh.

"Let's put it to the test." She stood. "Maybe you should try to walk out of the room."

"Wait!" Jett exclaimed. "Shouldn't we fix the portrait before he does that? What if he can't come back out because you've taken it apart?"

"True," Winston said. "That's a good point."

"Well, that shouldn't take long." Marleigh nodded at Jett. "Come help me."

Marleigh gathered up the portrait and took it to the kitchen table. The frame was still intact, but there were slight spaces in each corner where she'd pulled out the scriptures.

Jett pushed on each corner, closing the spaces and then placed the portrait back against the frame. Carefully, he replaced each staple in the holes where it had been removed. The portrait was a little loose from the frame when the task was completed, but it was together. "I hope this works," he said turning the portrait around.

"Well, I feel a lot better now," Winston said grinning. He walked towards the bedroom and disappeared.

Marleigh called him forth.

Once again, he came to her fully dressed in his uniform with his bear hat and sword. "Well, we know the spell hasn't been broken," he said setting down his hat and sword. He picked up the paper and read the scripture again, trying not to show his disappointment. He paused and looked up at Marleigh. "Do you have the poem? Maybe we missed something."

"I have it here." Marleigh held it up. She read it aloud once again and stared at Winston. "We read it together and in front of Jett. No Temperance appeared, and the spell hasn't been broken, so what are we doing wrong?"

Jett took the poem from her and silently read it. "If it's a spell, then maybe you should just read the words themselves and not the scripture references." He shrugged. "See what happens then?"

Winston looked at Marleigh. "Let's try it."

They began reading the scriptures leaving out the references.

"So if the son sets you free, you are free indeed," they read together and then looked around the room.

"Well done," a voice said though no one seemed to be there.

Without even thinking about what she was doing Marleigh called out, "Temperance, come forth."

Slowly, Temperance began to materialize right before their eyes.

"Temperance," Winston exclaimed stunned. "You're here. It worked! Is the spell broken?"

"It is," Temperance said smiling.

"Why are you smiling?" Winston asked suspiciously. "I would think you'd be angry."

"I was hoping that one day you would be free, so that I in turn would also be free. By imprisoning you, I myself was also imprisoned, though I didn't know it at the time the spell was cast. I didn't think about the consequences. You see, I was grieving the loss of my brother. I wanted to see him before he died, but your mother forbade it. Your father never told her about me, and because of his reputation, she didn't believe that I was his sister. Your father, Winston...was a bit of a rogue and it got him in trouble. Your mother had me tossed out. I was angry and when she died and her belongings were being auctioned by her estate, I bought the portrait of you. I wanted a portrait of your father, but there wasn't one. You looked so much like your father when he was your age; young and happy. Those were happy times for the two of us. I wanted to have a part of him with me always."

"Why was the gold in the portrait's chair?" Winston asked.

"I hid it from my son. Your father gave me that money over the years because our father refused to provide for me. I wasn't about to let Timothy gamble it away. Little Tim knew that I was a witch and I told him about the spell. He was just a boy and he believed, so I decided that when the time was right, I'd break the spell and give him the gold. I only wanted to keep you Winston, until the pain of losing your father lessened, but I got sick. I had to devise a way for the spell to be broken by someone other than by myself, because I realized that I didn't have long to live. There were rituals that must be performed in order to break the spell, but I was too weak."

"What did you do?" Marleigh asked.

"I had young Tim, my grandson, bring the painting to me while it was still wrapped in cloth, and I altered the spell as I lay on the bed. I wrote the poem, changed the rules and hid the pieces of parchment in the cracks, with Tim's help."

"How could you change the rules?" Winston asked. "I thought the rules were the rules. You always stressed that to me."

"Ah...well they are," she said smiling. "You see, I created the spell and I cast it, so only I could change it...or alter it as it was. I trapped you in there and you had to be freed by someone who also had been set free." She looked over at Marleigh. "Now, all of the conditions for the spell to be broken have been fulfilled, and I can rest in peace. Winston is free and now, he will age like any other man. He is no longer bound to the portrait."

"Your great-grandson was here," Marleigh informed her. "I have the gold."

"Do with it as you please," Temperance replied. "I know of all that has happened. He will not bother you again. Stealing the portrait has dire consequences."

"Will he die?" Winston asked.

"No, but a thief must pay penance with his hands," Temperance explained. "His hands will be of no use to him for the rest of his life. They will become crippled with arthritis. It has already begun."

Winston couldn't seem to feel sorry for Tim Rice as he pulled Marleigh closer. "I may be free, but I have no home, no identity. I have nothing to offer Marleigh. What good is being free, if I have no life?"

"Ah, but you do," Temperance replied as she walked over to the painting and touched it. She closed her eyes and touched Winston's shoulder then paused as if she were in a trance. "When you lie down to sleep tonight, you will wake up with new memories and a new identity." She then seemed to become transparent as a spark of light traveled from the painting through her and into Winston. "Now, it is time for me to leave you...I go now to my eternal rest. I too, am finally free." In an instant, she faded until she disappeared.

The quiet she left behind was interrupted by a shout from Jett, "Man, what a story!"

Epilogue

MARLEIGH LEANED OVER kissing Winston. "Wake up sleepy-head," she teased.

He opened his eyes, yawned and then smiled at her, happier than he could ever remember being.

A month had passed since the spell had been broken. She had introduced him to her parents, who both immediately commented that she'd found a live version of the soldier she had found at the yard sale. He had been nervous, but it didn't take long for him to win them over. They had told him that they could see that 'his nose was wide open'. He was still trying to learn American slang, but he had to agree with their assessment.

Just as Temperance had said, Winston had everything he needed to lead a normal life. He was now, Winston Spencer, born in Oxfordshire, England in 1995. He had an opportunity to come here to America on a working visa for the next two years. He remembered all of his previous experiences, but he now had new memories to go along with them. They had found luggage at the foot of the bed that next morning. Winston instantly knew it belonged to him. It contained papers for him to be in the country—just as Temperance had told them.

Winston realized he couldn't connect with his biological relatives, as he didn't really exist to them, anyway. His new memories had him growing up in an orphanage and going to University, followed by his joining the army. Everything had fallen into place, and he'd asked Marleigh to marry him. She had accepted without any hesitation.

The portrait still hung on the wall, but they'd moved it from the bedroom to the living room. Winston could barely stand to look at it, but Marleigh couldn't seem to part with it. So, he decided that when they moved to a larger place, he would find some out of the way spot to hang it.

Winston looked over at Marleigh who was running her fingers along his chest. He grabbed them and kissed them, smiling at her.

She stretched lazily in the bed and then pulled the covers up to her neck.

"Shouldn't you be getting ready for work?" Winston asked, quirking a brow.

Marleigh pouted. "I thought we could spend a little time together first."

"Ah," Winston replied pulling her into his arms. "I like the way you think."

Just then, the phone went off, interrupting their romantic moment.

Marleigh groaned. "It's seven in the morning, who could that be?" She picked it up.

Winston peeked at the caller ID to see it was Jett Graham.

"What do you want?" she snapped into the phone, not even greeting him. Putting the phone on speaker so Winston could hear the conversation, she grinned at him.

"Now Marleigh..." Jett laughed over the speaker. "I thought you'd want to be the first to hear about my new article. By the way, I want you to know that I appreciate you allowing me to send all ninety of those coins to Tim Rice, instead of shipping them one at a time."

"He'll need them for his medical expenses," Marleigh said, kissing Winston on the corner of his lip.

Winston snatched the phone from her. "Look here, mate. She is busy right now. Do not call here this early again." He then disconnected the call and tossed the phone back onto the nightstand.

"Well, that was rude," Marleigh said laughing.

"You want to see rude?" Winston grinned at her. "Climb on over here and I will show you something really, really rude."

"Oh, yes, my English gentleman. Be very, very rude to me," Marleigh said kissing him.

Made in United States
Orlando, FL
27 October 2023

38293943R00085